DREAMLINER

PRITHVI

Dedicated to

Lord SRI LAKSHMI GANAPATHI SWAMY

Contents

FOREWORD

Glancing at the night sky, we always see the moon, stars and the clouds with silver lining. Have you ever wondered why we focus only on heavenly objects in the sky while ignoring the dark background that holds all these wonders? May be that's how we are programmed or maybe that is how we learnt ever since childhood, or maybe that's was what mother taught us. And hence, we apply same to the life too. Focusing on sweet little things that happened every now and then in our life.

Imagine yourself sitting in balcony of your home while night breeze touching your hair quite gently, now gaze at the stars that are shining bright just as your eyes. Each star is like your memory, like memories make life, stars make the sky beautiful. This is exactly how I felt while reading each story in the book 'Dreamliner' penned by 'Prithvi'. Each story is a star.

In this busy life, when you find a moment for yourself, the little moments that holds your heart leaves you to feel ecstasy. Those moments are worth to live. That little moments, when you dance in shadows, when you find solace under tree, when you look at bird's nest can be re-visualized through lines in ' Dreamliner'.

Every living or nonliving in this universe holds a story to tell you, walls in the temple, indoor bonsai, windows at your work place and even the perfume bottle in almirah. Just as the narrative of Universe, narration of Prithvi about each article, situation and feeling that took birth in between is quite detailing with friendly language making it a perfect guide for your imagination.

"The roung big bindi with kumkum, that was the third eye. The bright eyes that always showered love, her beautiful smile as a symbol of peace...."

Is one such narrative of him about Goddess Kali Maa seems to be representing Maa in every woman.

As he narrates, "but a last photograph with the pigeons remained a memory", it reminds me of all the re-visting memories of mine that surfaced back to my eyes while travelling in between the lines of 'Dreamliner'. Trust me, you too will experience same joy when you meet your own memories through this amazing book. Did I forget to say that you'll miss a chance to meet all your childhood heroes if you missed a chance to grab this book?

I congratulate Prithvi along with showering my gratitude for giving a best place in paper boat to sail to the past... past with glitters and glimmers.

- Dr. Rama Sri Vineela Dasu

PREFACE

Reading as a hobby ripens into a habit with time. But writing cannot be taken as a simple challenge. Picking up a simple event and constructing story around has been a herculean task for past one year.

Most of the stories here are either true events or are inspired by incidents built up with some imaginary fictional descriptions. Some lost and forgotten incidents popped in my empty mind like 'The shadows I played with', 'Tora Tora', 'Perfume and the Gutter' which had an age of almost 20 years in my memory. Every story in this book had an inspiration from nowhere but everything around me. A small green leaf would catch my sight, a cool feather like breeze would draw my thoughts, a star in the sky would fly me away in imaginations, an exasperated acquaintance would trigger a story for me.

At some points, a visual in the vicinity would put me to a task to construct a story around it. A kid along with his father at a mango vendor, a banyan on the banks of a canal, a sultry noon at a beach where an eagle snatched a fish from the day's catch and a sketch of a man sleeping the terrace listening a radio under moonlight had been inspiration for almost 15 years to write an episode DREAMLINER, and that I insisted it'll be the title of the book.

Acknowledgements

Long hours of writing these stories would be far away from any possibility without any help of some modern gadgets. I'm grateful to possess a Dell Inspiron 15 for staying awake along with me till late hours and a portable speaker to plugin and play some cosy music to keep up my mood. Of course, sometimes a strong coffee also served the purpose.

I always had a privilege of friends who are quite a readers and I had a benefit of having my works reviewed by them. First, I should mention Rama Sri Vineela Dasu, who was constantly supporting me from the beginning and pushed me to publish my works. A ping from her would always carry information about a literary event or any update of her work or an inquiry about mine. Most part of our conversation would always be about our writings, a new book she or I liked, any new or post related to literature and poetry. A foreword from her to this book added a beauty. Her unselfish support and timely advises with her experience of publishing two books 'Intangible Tale' and 'Vibrant Tides' has made some of my tasks easy and efficient.

My friend Vamsi Kiran has also taken a task to read some of the stories to encourage me and put my targets high.

And I should not forget the dearest Narmada Varma for her support and the energy that she would permeate with me from time to time away from me or nearer. My love for her stands unvanquished at any moment.

What gadgets more do you need! My brother, Surendra presented me Apple iPad Air that allowed me to work on my writings at any place and time and, the small illustrations for every story and the book cover were designed on it. He is the first in the family to learn about my writing spirit and the foresaid gadget is just result of the belief he bestowed in me. I've once put one of his friends, Adarsh to a task to find a publisher for first timers and he readily came up with the answer.

A small thanks wouldn't fill my indebtness to them.

I

THE IMMORTAL

It is a morning in the monsoon, when the Sun is rising to touch the ground with its rays newly for the day, Ravi Chandran walked down the damp roads in the university campus to reach Godabarisha hostel to meet Srikanth. He hopped over shallow pits on partly damaged road carefully not to soil his track pants, but still he made his shoes dirt. Now, he carefully passed the sideways and cautiously opened the rusted gates and entered the compound and passed through the pathway sidelined by knee high grasses and few bushes. Now he was too careful to walk only to avoid slipping in the mud instead. The compound wall and the hostel were separated by a small undesigned garden with improper bushes, uncut grasses, some tall grown trees to widespread ones. Boundaries are lined with false Ashoka trees, some half grown. Some are teak, jamun and others randomly spread in the place. The thickness of green colour can be seen all over.

After cautiously walking on damp soil, he stepped on to the long corridor and headed to the end walking past the sky blue painted doors some locked and open, potted plants and a Ceylon creeper hanged by a jute rope. On left to the open side of the corridor clothes are hanged to dry, some giving away stink odour; not drying in the moist weather. The whitewashed walls have gone dim to the actual shade, patches of removed paint, bluish smudge at some places from top due to seepage from roof of the old building. A trail of ants crawling in discipline, door to door fetching the food. He reached the last room on the left wing no. 57 and found it was locked. Chandran looked to the other end of the corridor, long and with no sign of anybody moving around in the early hours of the day but some bollywood songs playing from a room on the far end. He took deep breath in and exhaled it strongly. He turned to the open side of the corridor and moved to stand at the edge facing the long trees and leaned over a pillar. Then he felt something pricking him through his track pants and saw a Ber plant, almost four feet tall and looked fresh with new flush. He then stepped back to keep away from its thorns and pulled phone from his pocket and dialed Srikanth, the phone is ringing inside the room, he sighed deeply and cut the call. He looked to at road, gate and again towards the room where songs were being played. He then moved to the other pillar and started playfully lifting leg straight to front and hitting the floor with the heel.

After few moments he noticed Bhakta Charan walking towards him singing, "Hai to hai to premara premara rangoli", stretched open his arms wide, tilting his head in rhythm with the tune and raising eyebrows singing loud his one if his favourites. He stood in front of Chandran still singing, now in high pitch. Bhakta has reached out for the keys put in the corner of closed window.

Bhakta guided Chandran, "Take keys from here whenever you come and carefully place it there again when you leave." Chandran replies with a yes.

"Be careful and if you drop the keys inside! We will have no option but to break the lock", Bhakta emphasized.

"Oh yes, sure."

Both entered the room and Bhakta turned on lights. This hostel is an old building of at least fifty years of age. It has high roofs and thick strong walls. The room is large and too much spacious to accommodate two people. It is very poorly lit with one tube light on one side and a CFL at one corner. Chandran lied down on Srikanth's bed and looking at Bhakta busy at his closet.

Bhakta took out a bundle of papers, rolled at their edges and corners, some folded and in uneven order. He placed them on bed and squatted. He handed some of them to Chandran and asked him to take a look. Chandran now sat properly and observed circles like scripture with strikes at some points and twisted lines in almost every word. Unable to understand the writings on those old papers, he sighed, "Hmm.. I don't know to read Odia, you knew it. Read it to me. I'll try to understand".

Bhakta took out a new set of papers in front of him, put his glasses right. Pursed his lips, took a deep breath, and exhaled it out strongly and short from mouth. Relaxed himself before reading it out.

He went on, "Ye tukhda tha, jo hamare dil se nikhla,..."

Bhakta finished his lines with a grin and fell silent for a moment. Then, Srikanth came back from his bath towel rolled around his slim waist, he removed slippers at a corner and stood under the ceiling fan to dry up himself. Lifting his chin up to see the slow rotating fan, he worried what would happen if the Earth rotated at that slow pace. He saw something was indifferent and silent. Both Chandran and Bhakta were looking at him and suddenly, they broke into mild laugh.

"Come on, now dress up quickly. Earth would never slow down its speed and neither Ramabai do", Chandran interfered his thoughts asking him to get for breakfast.

Srikanth left a deep sigh and put on clothes and moved out. Chandran's foot struck the floor slowly even slower than the ceiling fan while looking at the Ber plant that grew with green flush along the corridor. Pulling back his eyes from the plant, he walked along with Srikanth, crossed the hostel gates, and headed towards Ramabai's Tiffin Centre.

After returning from breakfast, Chandran and Srikanth stood at the door in the corridor. Chandran involuntarily moved towards the pillar and leaned on it again to find the pricking him through his track pants. He took a detailed look at the Ber plant, four feet tall with full flush of green. Leaves are short oval and some young leaves round shining in green with shorter stalks at very closer distance to each other and thorns that are amidst, but not longer than any leaf. The growth is nice and vigourous than normal plants. Their stem and branches are thin, dark, and young shoots in bright green. His eyes moved still lower, and he saw a thick woody trunk. This short bush, shining green in bright sun, caught his eyes to say something, something mystery!

Chandran shrugged his shoulders slightly, "How did this plant grow here? Very close to the wall, why don't you ask the labour to remove it?" his question came out very soft.

"Huh! This?" Srikanth sighed and replied, "It is plant immortal you know, cannot be removed so easily". Chandran astonished by his answer, lowered his brows and sunk his lips, "Immortal?" he questioned again.

"Yes, I had been seeing this plant for the last two years. Since I was accommodated in this hostel. It was removed several times but kept growing every time."

"Oh! Is it?"

"For the first monsoon, when we were admitted here, this tree was standing around six feet tall nice and green. Its branches grew well wide, like it was stretching its arms to open sky and two of them entered the corridor space also. The leaves were darker and larger than they are now", Srikanth continued, "This place was totally filled with grasses, bushes and other plants that would shelter poisonous reptiles. Then, at once our warden called in labour to remove all grass and small plants. The labour entered the garden wrapping their heads with short towels and some tied around their waist with all possible implements like spades, shovels, hoes, and sickles to destroy it. They all around the day and removed all that looked green with life except the big trees, piled them up and burnt after few days when they dried."

"Alright", Chandran gave a nod.

"This plant was cut till the level of ground. But it started to grow slowly after few days."

"Ok", Chandran is still listening with interest.

"Now, by the time winter started, all the grasses grew well and some bushes too. This Ber plant also grew to good height. Then some students in the hostel complained of mosquito's menace", Srikanth gave a small gap between his lines.

"Did they remove the plants again?" Chandran questioned.

"This time our warden engaged a small excavator that looked small and yellow with a hand in front to remove anything that came in its way and mouth like big tub on other side to swallow everything. Three big letters CAT were on the machine saying it Caterpillar make and looked to my eyes like a Bihar hairy caterpillar that ate all greens. It soon started its task to get the bushes removed, deep to their roots. The same was tried with the Ber plant. As it was too close to the building, they've cut it down to the ground, too deep this time but they couldn't remove the roots off. The labour didn't pile the grass and bushes, but left them as they were. Now, they'd put the fire and it has spread to the entire garden. I almost thought that the plant was dead and would never grow."

"Few days later, a month or maybe later I've seen small twigs shooting out and the Ber plant rising to life again. Let's hope that they'll let this plant grow into a full life tree", Srikanth concluded.

"That was great!" Chandran muttered slowly.

Chandran was pulled into his own pool of thoughts like he was thrown into a black hole. "Is it such a stubborn plant? It came across worst hurdles, but still growing green and new. It always started to grow new after every shock. It regained and lived"

"Yes, every time a tree is cut or felled; it leaves the lost part to its fate. It doesn't bother whether the removed part of the tree is burnt to ashes or utilised a timber or if carved into a wooden show piece or even if left to decay. It grows back into its own life. It rejuvenates back to form."

He is speaking with himself, "But why does man mull over his past, defeat, loss of anything. Doesn't recover and grow from the past to present and to the happiness in the presence of the instance. At this advanced state of human intelligence and sophisticated age, we run behind the past that has left us far behind. We do not look to outgrow from the defeat and the time that has moved away. We struggle over passing through hurdles."

"The advancement has pushed the man back to lower levels of intelligence. The must be immortal human souls are going to mortal state of being. There should be freedom from this."

Chandran came out from the black hole of his thoughts. He raised his eyes from the plant and looked through the blue door and that was dark inside. Srikanth has already gone into the room and he followed him and closed the door.

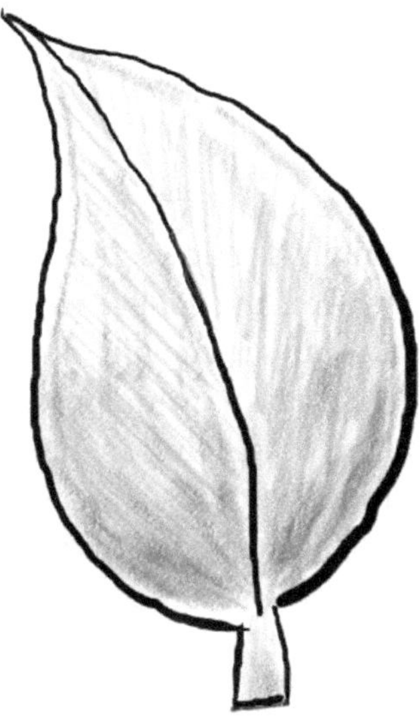

II

THE BONSAI

The time was 4.40 P.M., Sun is still shining bright and sharp rays entering through windows. All the buses ferrying students would have left the college premises by this time and residential students are moving around in the college farm and some going for an evening walk, to canteen and some of them might be playing in the ground. I was at my chair in staff room, and it is a great stress after taking classes for day long. I leaned back in the chair drawing my left foot onto chair seat, pushing it back fully and relaxing myself. Other chairs in the room are vacant. Pratap and Venkatesh, who sits to my left and right sides might be also at some place in the college. I still sat in the chair, closed my eyes, arms rested in lap and just trying to feel the air from ceiling fan. It is not comforting, but I felt like couldn't move. Then I heard some sound at the door. I lifted my head in sudden jerk. It is Anil from first year B.Sc. was standing there. I called him to come inside. He came to me and said that there is some workshop to be held and he wants to attend. I couldn't put any energy to hear him and asked him to come later in the evening to my hostel room.

I left the room after he went away and walked for a minute or two to reach the broken fence behind the college. There is a big barren land, a large space equals to the size of two football grounds, which is just vacant with some grass found at random spots and almost dried. There are some trees to the right side of my view that are merged with rocks stand high, that ineligible to call them a hill or too big to call boulders. And on the left side view, there is a big tamarind tree stretching some thousand arms and fingers to give big shade to enough to house my pleasure under it. I just looked around to confirm that I'm in no one's sight. Slowly, I crossed the fence and walked towards the tamarind tree. It even has a seating arrangement around it, some neatly shaped rocks were placed in two rows in a circle around the tree, at three meters from the tree trunk and soil filled in the gap. It is like a comfortable space to sit under its shade and experience the heaven. It's my usual space to spend some time alone. I neatly squatted there, opened top buttons of my shirt, and rested my arms on knees. Anyone seeing me from a distance might mistake me to be a yogi. Time passed unknowingly, when I was to get up, my left elbow is on knee and my jaw resting in the palm. A small stick is in my right hand that is writing some names and drawing figures in the soil that don't I remember. It is getting dark, and I walked back to the college building.

Straight away, I went to the staff room and collected my things packed and found few missed calls on my phone. They are from home and Pratap.

"Uff !", I sighed and slipped phone into pocket, took my laptop, books and went to the hostel room.

Now the time was quarter past nine, Pratap and I went for small walk after dinner and returned to hostel. Some students are still moving around and some of them are washing clothes at common utility taps. It is a common hostel building for students and faculty with a separate room for us.

As when we entered our room, the thing came to our sight is, Venkatesh is on his cot laying back to the headboard, stretching legs and as usually with mobile in hand placed on his large round tummy and scrolling down some stuff on Instagram. We both changed into night wear, Pratap has put on his lungi with big blue checks, and I changed into shorts and tees. We both are talking about casual things of the day and about the classes that must take tomorrow. Pratap is cracking some intermittent jokes on Venkatesh. I took out a novel from my shelf and sat on my bed laughing loudly. Pratap plugged in his mobile for charging. Then we heard a knock on the door. I guessed it would be Basheer, who comes late every evening after finishing his work. I went to open the door and it is Anil.

"Oh! Anil, it's you, come in."

He walked to my table slowly. I pulled a chair and asked him to sit. He is shy to sit comfortably. So, I held him by hand and made him sit. Then I inquired, "Huh..! You were saying something about some workshop or .... right? What is it"

He spoke in his slow voice, "S..Sir, tomorrow there is a workshop being held on... Bonsai Tree art. Some of us are interested in attending."

"How did you get the information about this?" I interrupted.

"Satya madam, she asked us to register", he gave a long pause.

Satya, she is the faculty of horticulture an active and enthusiastic lady. She keeps herself busy with some activity and students too. This keeps her searching for any workshops or training programmes that would be held nearby and registering students to them.

"What is the workshop about?" Pratap entered the conversation. He is often curious about the things around him. He should be given the desired information sooner, or else the heat of the atmosphere rises.

"S...sir, Bo... Bonsai Tree art", Anil stuttered.

"What is the venue?" Pratap questioned again.

"Sir, some hotel near Uppal", Anil replied.

"How many of you are attending? What is the registration fee and all?" I asked him.

"Ten of us are attending and the fee is Rs. 900 per participant for two days and ..."

Meanwhile in between the conversation, Ashok entered the room along with Ram calling us, "Sir, good evening." Pratap immediately warned them to remove footwear at the door. Ashok stopped at once raising his hands in air and obstructing Ram's way, "Oh! Oh! Okay sir."

Now both of them joined the talk and repeated the details.

"Huh! Okay, now is it going to be a two day training or an outing for you guys?" I asked with a witty smile.

"I think, these people registered only to skip the college for two days, isn't it?" Pratap joined me. Three of them left the room after some lighter conversation.

It's been two days and these guys were not seen in the college. They used to leave the campus leisurely at nine o'clock in the morning and reach at five o'clock or later in the evening.

Then the third day morning I came early to the campus, marked my attendance and went to ladies' staff room in the ground floor. Nobody has come yet. As soon I entered the room, I found a pot on Satya's table and a small stout plant in it. It is the Bonsai and something around it caught my attention. I went towards Ms. Kulkarni's table to place my books and returned to check the Bonsai. It is too short that it should be called plant, but it looks like an aged one and I'm confused to call it a Bonsai plant or tree.

It is stout and the girth is thick, small leaves that are little round in the size of green peas and placed sparsely. The plant looked woody and the bark also like an aged plant. The main element that caught my attention and that worried me is the GI wire that was wound around the trunk and twisted till the tips of the branches constricting its growth and forcing it to be smaller than usual. There are two GI on it, a thicker one wound around the main trunk to the apex and big branches; a thinner one running around small branches. Those GI wires sprouted out from the soil mix in the pot. I lifted it and found that they ran all through the pot and came out from the drain hole at the bottom and twisted tight to the hold the Bonsai in place and keep it from growing against the gravity.

Then, Satya came from behind and patted on my shoulder asking how the Bonsai is. I expressed my disappreciation. But she didn't care my remark. I asked why the Bonsai is made to take with these iron wires. Then she took the pot from my hands and explained me that these wires are used to bring the Bonsai to the desired shape we want and train it the way we wish to see.

"Do you know different types of Bonsai? We need to train them using these wires to acquire the shape. These wires also hold the roots in restricted position to slow down the growth and bring stunted nature. Soil is changed at timely intervals and training of the roots is also checked", I am listening her brief explanation and didn't like the idea of Bonsai in any way.

The ancient Chinese art of growing dwarf trees in small earthen pots and containers adopted new techniques to take new form and continue its legacy. But it stunted a life form and has put it bounded in size and shape.

I remembered once our English teacher in class five narrating a poem on Bonsai and that gave me a picture of how a Bonsai looked. I don't exactly remember if the author had praised the dwarf nature of Bonsai, pitied is it. He described it beautifully and the happiness when he achieved in making a perfect Bonsai. He also described the pain that the plant would be put to bring out such an art work.

"What is the age of this Bonsai?" I enquired about the tree which is not more than a foot and few inches tall.

"Aah..! They said it'll be three years old."

"Hmm. Maybe it should be allowed to grow to its fullest form. The Bonsai maybe an art, but stunting one's life is not a life, Satya."

"You are obviously right my brother. But still, it is an art from ancient times."

"Okay. Maybe this creature on this Earth was destined to live this way."

III

A BROKEN NEST

I returned from office by 5.30 in the evening, mom was sitting in the living room. I straight away went to clean myself, put my lunch box in kitchen sink, kept the backpack in my room. I was heavily sweating that my shirt is too wet, and I look like bathed. When I changed my clothes and getting ready for a bath, mom called me to tell about the bird's nest that she had seen in the garden. She called me out to the balcony and pointed out at the hibiscus plant where, under the cover of the leaves, there is a small nest. Mom said that there were three small eggs in oval shape, brown colour and white patches over it. It was already dark, and I couldn't notice anything.

After a few days, when I came retuned from office, mom said that the eggs hatched, and three small baby birds were in the nest. That evening when servant maid came for her work, she suggested that we shall put some grains into their mouths and feed them. But mom warned her not to think of anything like that, "They're small baby birds, how do you expect them to feed on grains?"

After listening to mom's findings, I inquired, "What birds are they?"

"I don't know. They're dark with red tinge and barely hairless", mom replied.

"Hmm. Let's see tomorrow", I said and went away.

That next morning, I woke up late and didn't even think about the birds as I would be late to office. Then later in the evening as soon I came back home, I parked the bike and took my phone and approached the nest. It was small nest built with dry grass blades and brown colour, slightly larger than a half cut cricket ball standing on a juncture of three branches on hibiscus plant.

I turned on the camera and extended my arm towards the nest. Then I observed two things. As my hand touched the branch and disturbed it slightly, the baby birds lifted their heads up, stretched their mouths open and rotating their heads expecting their mother to put some food. Very true form of love that the babies, though they are blind to see their mother still long to find her. Secondly, their mother is actually sitting on the electricity service wire that is just above and squeaking loud and continuous. The blind expectation to find one and a terrible fear loose one. The two ends of love are at sight.

I switched my vision up and down from the mother and the baby birds. The three heads are moving with open mouths like they were triggered by some key and the mother is also looking up at the other bird that stationed itself just a yard's length away.

"Oh! There is another bird. I must move away quickly", I said to myself.

I clicked three pictures quickly and slipped out. They were just enough to identify that they are birds and their wide open mouths. I showed the pictures to mom and later to father after he returned from office.

Later at night, I remembered about the birds and thought if I would take out the DSLR to photograph them. But I felt that it'll not be a good idea to frighten those tinies with zooming lens.

Next morning, a crippled idea came to my mind. Why wouldn't I just take a video of the birds and share it to my friends.

"How creepy I'm?" the later feeling at the end of the story.

I immediately grabbed the mobile phone, put on my tees, and sped downstairs. I straight away walked towards the hibiscus plant and approached the half cut cricket ball. They are lying in the nest with one's head on the other and cuddling each other. I was looking into the nest while the morning sunlight's heat was irritating me. Then I heard the elder mother bird squeaking over my head. I again moved out quickly, camera on and a short video clip in the phone. I quietly came out and first shared the video clip to a close friend of mine and then to a group of my colleagues next.

Few days passed on and I was observing the half cut cricket ball every day from a safe distance and the tinies are growing well. It was all good. Once, mom mentioned that she went to garden to take flowers or bring some curry leaves and she found that the baby birds were actually flying. They flew to a short distance from nest to the fence and back. This turn, the mother bird had shown its aggression. It suddenly came over mom's head like it'll attack her. She moved away quickly to safety.

That next day as soon I returned from work, father called me that we will take a small video of the birds. I hesitated to disturb them and called it a bad idea, but agreed later still condemning the act. Then we both went down to the garden. Dad moved in first and I followed him. I cautioned him to keep away and not to touch the plant, as there would be any risk of the birds flying away. Still, he went near the nest and tried moving a branch for a clearer view.

The unexpected happened. Just in the shock of the moment, the baby birds suddenly flew from the nest and landed on the fence just two yards away. The sky is now getting darker quickly. There is a flash of lightening far away and heavy force of wind came in. And in the blink of the eye, these baby birds flew away from the garden and stood on the cut and felled branches of the bushes in the opposite vacant site. Now we noticed the tussle between the parent birds. Father bird brought himself into fight with his mate. They flew to the ground and the male bird was just running behind the female aggressively and squeaking loudly. The female bird jumped from one place to other trying to escape the attack. It suddenly flew down to ground and missed its balance and cupped its wings on the floor, it looked like an act of fear and fight. It was so furious, and I opened my eyes wide in shock. Among this flashing and fearful moments, we couldn't find where the young birds have flown away. Dad and I were standing at the gate looking all round. After the furious act, the parent birds flew towards the bushes to find their young ones. They jumped from bush to branch and tree, but in vain. When the evening kept growing darker, those birds too vanished in the camouflage.

It is about to rain, dad and I moved back into house. It was a desperate moment. I even hesitated to look towards dad. But he was unhappy too. He never expected or wanted it to happen that way. I stood in the verandah looking at the dry bushes. A light rain started to touch the ground, very light and it didn't last long. Just some fast winds and thunder strikes far away. It just gave me a hope that babies would be safe on any tree or a bush.

That next morning was Sunday. I was leisure as usual as every Sunday and went on a light walk to get some milk and newspaper. All along the way I was walking, my eyes were searching every tree to find any sign of the baby birds. I searched them on my way back too. I've put the milk pouches on kitchen platform and came down again to search if there were struck under the bushes.

I went around the dry bushes that were lying in the vacant site in front of the house. I was looking into everything lying there. I pulled out some dry branches to get a clear sight under them, took a stick in hand to lift any plastic or paper or any litter that could probably hide the tinies. I went back to half cut cricket ball that was empty now. Stood there facing and trying to figure out the possible points where the young birds could fly with their underdeveloped wings. After guessing one or two spots, I searched again and no result.

While I was going from one point to other, coming back the nest and going again, the parent birds appeared. The mother bird was carrying some termites in its mouth and father bird made some fierce sounds again. I looked at them for a moment, sighed and came back to bushes and looked out for them around and at possible places. The sunshine was bright that day and I was sweating heavily. The sun was getting brighter and hotter. So, I left the task their and came back to home. I was moving around in the house, but with heavy heart. Father asked me if found them. I gave a little serious reply and moved away. He was sad of course, but the thing done cannot be reverted.

I went to my room soon and shut the doors for some privacy for few hours. Turned on my computer, plugged in headphones and played some favourite classicals. The parent birds were seen moving around till the next day and the half cut cricket ball nest disappeared in some wind. There was a cyclonic depression in the Bay of Bengal, and it rained heavily for few days and no sign of the birds. Later, the bushes were removed on a fine day. The topic of the baby birds subdued. But whenever, birds come into my sight, I remembered the day when the baby birds were lost and got separated from their parents.

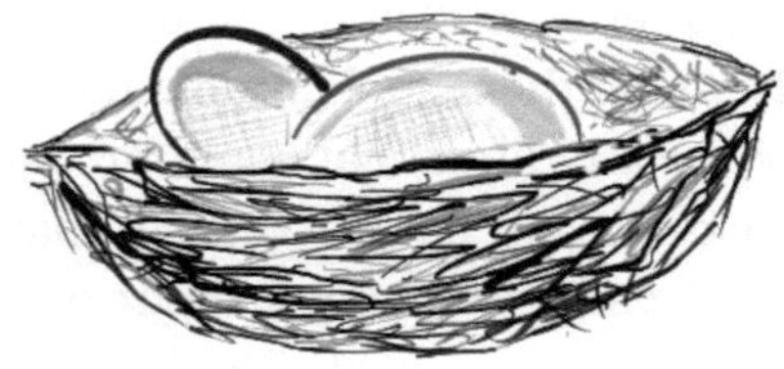

IV

THE SHADOWS I PLAYED WITH

I was at my grandmother's house for a weeklong holiday. Holiday at grandparent's house is just overwhelming to spend the time timelessly. Late night talks with grandfather and grandmother, silly plays with Somu uncle, lazy mornings, and happy smiles. Even regular meals tasted like heaven (my grandmother has herself taught my mom to cook, but food here is different). Waiting for the evening snacks that my grandfather would bring for us was like more than anything. My brother Gopal and I should be thankful to my mother for readily accepting our request.

Both of us had a great time for entire holidays. We used to play running around the garden, climbing trees to pluck some guavas, swing like monkeys, we would fight and hit each other in leisure times when there is nothing to play but to offend for no reason. Somu uncle would sometimes take us on a cycle ride whenever he took off from his classes.

Five days passed on without any notice of time. We had two more days to finish our holiday and mom would come the next day to shower some love on her mother and take us back with her to home. It will be like a suffering to attend school after an awesome holiday we had for a week. It was Saturday and we've already laid our demand for a country chicken curry for Sunday and grandfather was deployed on this work.

Then the evening approached very calmly with pleasant breeze and carrying some dust along with it. We had already had some milk and light snack and sat in the long verandah. Grandma was looking towards the road for Grandpa and Uncle to return home. Weather is changing rapidly, skies getting darker, and wind picked up its speed now lifting all the sand and dust on the roads along with dry fallen leaves. Now the wind is getting robust, it carried all the sand and dust into the house. Grandma asked us to get inside the house and now she is more worried about Grandpa and Uncle to return soon before it gets worse. By the time it started to rain, and the black clouds started to make noise in the sky. Grandma noticed both Grandpa and Somu uncle approaching quickly. Yes, of course they both are also worried of getting stuck in the rain and windstorm. Grandma sighed heavily and exhaled a deep heavy breathe as sign of relief.

As soon they came in, Grandma inquired of how bad the weather was though she had been witnessing. She gave them towels to wipe their damp hair and facilitated to make themselves comfortable. By the time Grandpa and Uncle settled down, the power supply was cut off.

"Uff.. Why there is a power outage now!" Somu Uncle sighed.

Grandpa sat silently in his place and Grandma gave them both some refreshments and brought candles. She has lit two of them and placed one on the tea table and another in the kitchen. Grandma has started preparation for evening supper in very dim lit kitchen. Many sounds from utensils clinking to filling water in bowl to cook rice, spoons dropping on the floor, cutting vegetables, lighting the gas stove, and mixing up vegetable in the hot utensil to make a curry, all were heard in the silence of the evening after rain. Slowly, few moments later, a tasty mouthwatering flavour reached our nostrils.

In the presence of dim light, everything fell in silence and my grandfather's senses worked very well. He called Grandma in the kitchen and asked about the luring food that she is preparing for all of us.

"It is for the kids. They like potato fry with kasuri methi and lemon to add tangy flavour. Of course, you'll have your share too", replied Grandma.

"Your mother always cares about her daughter and her kids. She least thinks about us." Somu uncle gave a small grin in reply to Grandpa's so called sarcasm.

"Huh... Isn't she your daughter? This old man's nasty joke", Grandma went away into kitchen.

Meanwhile Gopal and I sat near the candle, and he showed me some tricks that he had learnt from his friends. Firstly, he passed his finger from the candle flame without burning himself and not letting the flame go off. I was just surprised as it is the first time I'd ever seen. When I tried to do the same, he stopped me saying that I may burn my hand.

I sighed and shrugged hesitatingly, "I'll try once, only once."

"No. You'll burn your hand. It is not easy for you", he stopped me again.

He continued repeat it again and again, I was looking at him. Once I lifted my head up to see the roof ceiling, I observed a big shadow of his hand, moving from one end of the ceiling to opposite end. I looked down towards his hand, it is very small here that it could hold only a cricket ball in its fist. But, on the roof top ceiling its shadow seemed so big that it can hold the ceiling fan, four foot long tube light would feel like a half broken pencil in it, I also felt like all the four remaining people in the house could sit on his palm, if it is really this big.

Then I had placed my hand a little above the flame and the shadow of my hand too looked bigger. Then I twisted my fingers round like I was making a whirlpool and that felt like I would churn if whole room were filled with water.

Then I stood against the candlelight and found myself in the size of a monster on wall as a shadow. That was amazing and Gopal pulled the tea table to one end of the room for the candlelight to be projected on a plain wall. We both stood against the light and again appeared as shadow monsters on the wall. I moved my body in different ways and danced there seeing how my shadow appeared. I walked to and from the candlelight and observed that my shadow got bigger and smaller. The size of shadow monster changed. We both became Lilliputs and the Giant like in the Gulliver's travels at the same time.

I brought some small toy cars and others placed them against the light. We both played hitting each other's toy cars and G.I. Joe toys. Then Gopal showed me something else to do with fingers and transform light into animal and bird like shadows. He touched the tips of his middle and ring fingers with the tip of thumb to make a tear drop shape and lifted the index and little finger, that looked like a young deer. His other hand also came the same way and made movements like the deers moving one after another and then turned their heads opposite to each other and kissed.

"Hehehe..", I laughed and repeated with him. This time, the deer I brought had a fight with Gopal's.

Now he closed his fist and inserted one pencil between the index and middle fingers, another between the ring and little fingers. He made a zigzag wriggling movement and said it is a caterpillar. Then came rabbit, he stuck out his index and middle finger and held thumb out. He held out his right palm facing wall and left hand facing top like holding a bowl, this also made a deer but with horns.

Now he brought two cricket balls and asked me to assume the candle to be sun and delivered his knowledge on solar and lunar eclipses. I placed my head in my uplifted palms and listened to him. He rotated the balls round the candle and showed me some shadows. Then finally after a fews minutes of playing, I felt sleepy and yawned. Grandma asked us to call off our play to have dinner and sleep.

After the dinner, Grandpa, Somu uncle, Gopal and I sat in the sit out looking towards the damp street, dim glowing streetlights that blinked intermittently and some adult termites that emerged after a rainy evening and flew around the light only to drop off their wings and disappear. Slowly and unknowingly, I slipped into sleep.

When I woke up in the morning to sharp sunlight entering the bedroom, I was next to Gopal who is still asleep. All that happened last evening was still live in my memory and I went to the living room. The candle was placed in a small steel cup. Grandma would always light candles and place them in this cup and after years of that practice, the cup was filled with wax from various candles in different colours. The candle that was lit last evening is now almost burnt and only small piece of it is seen with a small wick.

Grandma saw me at the tea table and said, "Chaitu, brush your teeth quickly and take bath. Your mom called just a moment ago and she will be coming soon. Wake up Gopal too."

"Okay!!"

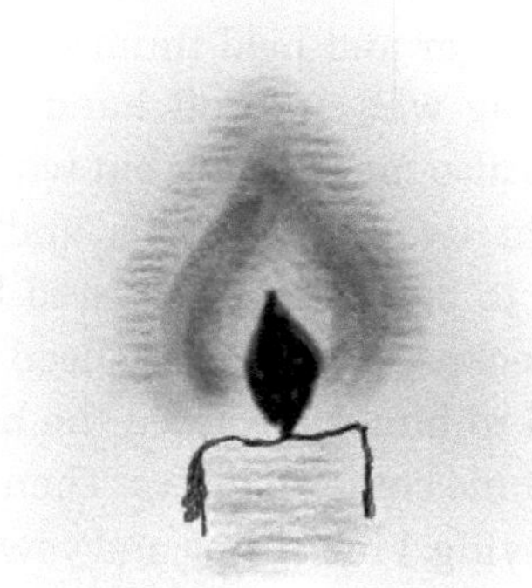

V

AMRUTH AUR KACHHA AAM

Nithin is drawing lines with his finger on the glass shelves of the fancy store. He is trying to draw a battery operated white limousine that is displayed in the shelf, he is figuring out the Spiderman which is just after the limousine and the round toy drum. The store is just colourful, glittery, shining with glossy surfaces and bright toys, gift articles and show pieces. Nithin's eyes caught a short yellow colour soft toy, it is bald with big round big eyes and big funny smile in blue dress. It is a character from the movie Minions, which never spoke a language that is understood.

Just then Swathi called him, "Nithin beta, come here."

"Mumma see that Minion, it is nice. Please take that for me, I want it."

"Not now. Come on take this candy", she handed him a kachha mango (raw mango) candy that the shop keeper gave instead of change. He looked at the candy that his mom gave him. It is a dark green colour wrapper and raw mango picture in light green colour. Stepping out of the shop, he opened the wrapper and put that mild green colour translucent candy in mouth. He didn't like it, but he didn't spit it out. Swathi also had one candy with her and she popped it in. Due to the sudden sour taste, she twisted her mouth drawing her jaws in and closed eyes.

"Ah! It's too sour. Nithin, did you like it?" She questioned him.

"Naah!"

"Ohw! Did you sulk on me now?"

"Nah!"

"Haha.. Short reply again, cutie we'll buy that Minion some other time."

Nithin did not give any reply. He spitted out the half eaten candy. They both walked back to home. By the time they home, Arjun is watching TV and Nithin suddenly climbed into his father's lap.

"What did you buy?" Arjun asked Swathi. "She didn't buy what I need", Nithin complained about his mom.

"What did you ask to buy?"

"I asked Mom to buy a Minion soft toy for me", Nithin shrunk his face and expressed hesitation.

"It's ok Nithin, we are unable buy now. But I'll surely buy one for you and a bigger one. Okay?" Arjun cajoled his sulking son. "Did she not buy you a chocolate or candy?" he asked Nithin.

"Yes, mom gave me a raw mango candy. Nobody may find it is a raw mango candy nevertheless told."

"Hahaha", Arjun and Swathi laughed in unison.

Swathi prepared dinner for three of them and called both father and son to dine.

The next day morning, Swathi got the tiny tot readied for school and Nithin wore his small red and white checked shirt and crimson red short pants for school uniform. Swathi served breakfast for both Arjun and Nithin. And then Arjun left for his office, Swathi dropped Nithin at his school.

It is 12.30 in the afternoon, and it is time for Nithin to leave school. He came outside waiting at gate for his mom to pick him. But for his surprise, Arjun came to pick him up from school. In a blink of the eye, he stopped his bike in front of Nithin. Nithin is all smiling after his father's approach. Nithin climbed up the bike behind his father and circled his arms around Arjun's belly. Nithin is pumped up with joy to have a bike ride though it'll be a short one just till home. But Arjun drove the bike in another direction from their house. Nithin is more joyous now and asked Arjun where they are going, "Pappa, where are we going?"

"Just till the end of the street, we'll buy fruits. One of my friends is visiting our home in the evening today."

"Oh! Who are they?"

"Avinash uncle and Anitha auntie. Do you remember them?"

"Ah!", after a gap, "maybe, I can recognize if I see them."

And within two minutes, they reached to an outlet of a fruit vendor and Arjun bought some grapes and mangoes. They Nithin pointed towards a lady who is selling guavas by footpath. Arjun has taken him there and bought a dozen of them. But, what actually Nithin wanted was raw mangoes that she sells besides guavas.

"I want kacha aam Pappa", Nithin laid his demand.

Then Arjun asked the lady to give him some cut pieces of a raw mango.

That lady looked carefully towards the pile of mangoes. She had already sensed Nithin's craving for a juicy, sour and a little sweet tingly mango. She has moved some mangoes in the basket and took out a nice raw mango, evenly greenish with small white spots, nice and curvy, glossy and handful to catch. She felt the mango in her hand and decided it will have a right punch of taste. Then, she wiped the fruit with a clean cloth and held it in left hand, took a sharp knife to slice it up into pieces. She has cut the mango smoothly into slim long pieces. The flesh inside was in light yellowish creamy colour, looked nice and moist. Then, she finished slicing the mango and placed the slices on piece of paper that was already kept ready. The sour sweet flavour filled the vicinity of the vendor lady. Nithin sniffed deeply to fill his nostrils with the flavour. The sense of smell gave him a small jerk that he felt like not the smell sense, but mango itself has got into his brain. That vendor lifted her gaze towards Nithin to witness his happy smiling face and she too smiled a little.

Now, the lady held a round plastic box in left hand that has two partitions filled with chilli powder and salt to sprinkle on the mango slices. She took a pinch of salt with three fingers and just moved them against each other, and the tiny salt crystals dropped on to the slices. She did this in rhythmic patterns. The salt crystals that fell on the slices sticked to the moist juicy surface and some melted to get absorbed into fleshy mango. Some crystals bounced and fell off the slices.

Then she took chilli powder and slowly sprinkled on each slice. That fine powder got stuck on the very moist mango slices and gave a mouthwatering view to little Nithin who is waiting to taste them soon. That crimson red colour for chilli powder, light yellow colour of flesh and the green skin of raw mango were feast to Nithin's eyes. That lady took utmost care not to add too much hot pepper and irritate the little champs taste buds. Now, she handed the mango slices to Nithin and took money from Arjun.

Both of them walked away from there and Nithin held the slices in one hand and took the first piece into other. He smelled the sour and a little sweet flavour of the raw mango. He sniffed the sharp, strong and pungent chilli pepper sprinkled on it. Now slowly he introduced the flavour to his taste buds. He licked it a little and took a small bite of it. That sour taste of raw mango, he shook with a joy. And then with the hot pepper and salt that tickled his tongue, he exclaimed, "Ah!"

He took all the juicy bites one after the other and the other. He grinned widely looking at his father. Arjun responded back with a smile. He offered Arjun a piece in his hand, and he took one and that hot pungent odour and sour taste that twitched his jaws. Arjun closed his eyes to feel only the tasty raw mango, but nothing for the moment. They finished up eating two slices each carried two for Swati. She is waiting for them to arrive, but there is a heavenly thing waiting for her in the little hands of Nithin.

VI

MOTHERHOOD

"Hufff... uuh!", Sampath stretched his body after a long post lunch nap. Summer afternoons quickly let you fall asleep after a nice meal. Of course, it is Sunday and he had a nice square meal. Still lying on divan (a couch with mattress, that more looks like a small bed), he looked at the wall clock overhead. It is almost 4:15 PM and turned towards his mom, Mrs. Kamakshi working on her sewing machine and looking outside through the main door. And there is an unusual expression on her face. Her frowned eyebrows and deep curled forehead. Sampath worried about what has happened and asked his mother with a concern, "Mom, what happened? Why are looking so serious?"

She has now made a normalized expression on her face and spoke to him, "The maid has not come today also."

"Oh! Is that it? Why should you be so serious about this and hurt yourself?"

"You don't know boy. This has become a habit for her to skip a day or two every time or come too late and later plead for an excuse. She doesn't even clean properly and having no choice of any other maid, I have to adjust with her work."

Mrs. Kamakshi was serious about the maid that Sampath felt that is really a matter of concern. So, he asked her one more question, "How much do we pay her?"

"Six hundred rupees a month. That's only to clean the verandah in ground, first floor and in front of the gate."

"How do they get paid in general?" he raised one more question.

"The other maids get paid only a thousand for serving a building of two or three floors. We comparatively pay her well", she replied to him.

Then at around 4.30 PM Mrs. Kamakshi has seen Shanthamma coming all the way carrying her two year old kid in arms. She looked too lean and poorly brushed hair that has turned light brown and she looked unclean after working in many other houses. Her kid whom she carried in her arms looks like he soiled his clothes and hair and caught all the dirt he could while playing. Both the mom and son looked pale brown.

Shanthamma drops her child from her arms carfully and caught the broom, and he immediately started to cry with a loud noise. She tried to calm him down, but he gave no other choice but to carry him along. She again lifted him in her left arm and started to broom the floor with the right. She spoke to him with care and love expressing her tiredness, "Why don't you get down and let mom do her work. We'll finish quickly and go home after this." But he waved his head in disagreement, but spoke nothing.

Then Mrs. Kamakshi asked Shanthamma why she has come too late. Shanthamma tried to give some sort of inappropriate explanation that did not convince her. Then Kamakshi gave the boy few cookies to eat, "Here Ganesh, take these biscuits and sit there. Your mom will finish her work and come back quickly."

But he waved his head in disagreement again. Then Kamakshi made a serious note and at once he got down from her arms and sat quietly munching on his biscuits.

Shanthamma then cleaned the verandahs and sprinkled a bucket full of water in front of the gate that is mixed with cow dung and brought small plastic container with lime powder in it. She has put some dots on the wet ground in calculated number. Then drew some nicely curved zigzag lines around the dots, some circled at the corners, finally joining all the lines leaving no clue where she actually started. This made a simple South Indian rangoli that could be found at every house in villages. Mrs. Kamakshi insisted on this simple rangoli even after living for so many years in a city, as it brought some beauty to the home, and it looks serene.

Shanthamma lifted her son with one hand, brought him in her arms and walked away. This boy in her arms is her third child. She carried him seating on her waist, walking weakly with low pace. She reached home found the eldest of her kids Mallesh and daughter Swapna playing with the other kids. She called Mallesh and handed him a ten rupee note and asked him to get some potatoes from nearby vendor. Then she remembered that rice wouldn't be sufficient for the supper and called him back to give forty more rupees and purchase rice at Hakim's general stores.

Shanthamma allowed Ganesh to play with other kids and she made herself clean and tidy then went to her sister who lives in the adjacent house with her two daughters. Both of them spoke their hearts out and relaxed until her brother-in-law came in. She then left to her house. Mallesh has returned by that time and left the potatoes and rice in the corner of the kitchen and went away to play.

Shanthamma found the potatoes and a packet of rice at the corner of the kitchen place. Soon she took some rice into a bowl and called her daughter Swapna to peel potatoes and slice them, "Swapna. Swapna...! Come here and peel these potatoes."

Swapna obeyed her mom's order and left the playing crowd. She took a knife from the old wooden cupboard in the corner. It was given to Shanthamma by an old lady for whom she worked a year ago. Shanthamma keeps her every month's earnings inside the cupboard to hide it from her husband and Swapna is the only one who knew this secret.

Soon Swapna peeled the potatoes, sliced them into small pieces then chopped two onions and some green chilli. She brought these vegetables and handed them to her mother. Shanthamma cooks on firewood stove that she has built in the verandah place with clay mud and dapped with dung. Swapna seeing her mother struggling to lighten up the firewood, she took the blowing pipe into her hands and blew the air with force and built up the fire.

"Mom, why don't we buy a gas stove? That will be easy to light and cook. You don't have to struggle like this every time", Swapna asked her mother.

"We cannot afford a gas stove child. It is a costly affair to our family and our expenses. And if any houses and apartments are built all over these surroundings and all the trees are felled, we wouldn't get this firewood anymore. Then it'll be necessary to switch over to a gas stove."

Swapna sighed deeply and stood up to leave. But Shanthamma asked her to sit along with her. "When should you leave for school?"

"Next week maybe", Swapna replied reluctantly.

"See child, I had to keep you and your brother away from home is only for your good future and wellness. Here, I cannot afford you a good nutritious food or clean clothing. And your education will be better in a welfare association hostel. Your uncle also stays nearby. So, he can take care of you both."

"Hmm... but I want to stay with you mom. I'll have you to my company", Swapna spoke in a sad voice.

"You know about your father. What a man he is! It is not safe for you to stay along", Shanthamma sighed.

Shanthamma then remembered the days just before her marriage. How she was forced to marry Nagu, her elder sister's husband after her death only to save her family from the debts incurred by her father. People also believed that it is his plan to get his first wife to death and he would stand a chance to marry Shanthamma. The young healthy woman was found dead, hanging to a ceiling fan one morning in her house and her husband pretended as he knew nothing and didn't allow anyone to file a case with the Police saying it would attract untoward consequences and convinced the village heads with the same. Being a remote hamlet village, her death went unnoticed by any officials.

Nagu has an eye Shanthamma even before marrying her elder sister Ganga. He used to bully her sometimes and tried to make advances towards her before and after marrying Ganga. Shanthamma has to resist him and kept her mouth zipped always to save her sister from being tormented by the moron. But dices of the fate always rolled in the favour of Nagu. After few months of Ganga's death, Nagu approached Shanthamma's parents to get her married to him. So, that they would get rid of the debts and would also save on the budget of marrying Shanthamma to someone else. The poor family has got no other choice at the moment.

Later, the couple moved to the nearby city and Nagu worked as contract labour in an industry. Shanthamma has no good living condition here. He was good to her only for few months and then he switched to his devilish actions. Though Shanthamma never had a good opinion towards him, she has to do her duty as a wife. Then she chose to work as servant maid at few houses to earn a living that will keep her children and her from starving.

Shanthamma made a brief account of her past to Swapna and asked her to keep a good track of education and then buy her a gas stove when she will start earning for herself. She smiled and went away.

Nagu returned home late, children were already asleep by that time. That drunkard has come over to Shanthamma and shamelessly asked her to satisfy his lust tonight. She then refused his advances and pushed him away. But he continued to force her into the action. After few requests he slapped her on the face and pushed her down on to the floor. Children woke up to the noise, but feared to make any sound or move a little. He pulled her to his convenience and continued to work with his lust and a few moments later released himself from his desire. The thing Shanthamma could do only is to moan in pain, when the man left in his pleasure.

That next day she was behaving all normal and let the children not notice any of her inconvenience. She has prepared some food for the breakfast and fed her children. Then she left for the day's work.

The first house she would work for is Mrs. Ratham's. A two storeyed building, where she would clean all the house and wash utensils. Mrs. Ratham offered her a little respect but heavy work. Then to the second house of Mrs. Lakshmi. She is a good, generous lady and spoke well to everyone. She would treat Shanthamma well but, less satisfied with her work. Yes, of course Shanthamma never puts her efforts in doing work that would leave her payers in dissatisfaction. She did this only to cover most of the houses in less time and earn few hundreds more that could feed her children with good food and sufficient clothing. Then she would go to work in a restaurant kitchen, where she has a pile of utensils to wash. Here, she is paid well and there is a least check on how she cleans the oiled and used utensils. Shanthamma returns home after taking food in the kitchen that is left as excess. All the three children will have their food and wait for their mother to come. She sometimes would bring some food from the kitchen to keep it for the supper and sometimes any tasty delicacies as the children would enjoy them.

Shanthamma would always work at different places to earn a living and tolerated some hardships only keep her children away from hunger and give them good clothing and facility. This is the promise that she has made to herself.

VII

DREAMLINER

Bhargav has just taken a hot shower and relaxed himself after a day's long work. He was waiting for a hot coffee to stimulate his senses to start his evening. Then his wife, Prashanti called him, "It may take long to boil the milk and make a coffee, why don't you go to the wait on the terrace? I'll get you coffee and some snacks."

Then Bhargav stood up from the couch and stretched his body to right and left and bent forward relieving the pain. "Aah.! This is good." He exclaimed and went upstairs. He looked around for the foldable cot and found it placed against the parapet wall. Then he brought it to the middle of the open terrace, unfolded and dusted it. It is an iron framed cot painted in blue and woven with a cloth patti. Now he just lied down on the cot and looked towards the sky, the only unending roof above him. Bhargav used this foldable cot when he was a bachelor and stayed just a few streets across from the present house. He had to put it away as it wouldn't be a sufficient for his wife and him together. But he tends to lay down on that cot on terrace to relax and enjoy some leisure evenings and peaceful talks with his beautiful wife. Sometimes he falls asleep there itself and Prashanti calls him back into the house.

A few minutes later, his beautiful and dutiful wife brought a hot coffee for Bhargav and a cup of tea for herself and some snacks in a plate. Bhargav smiled at her and sat up to give her some place along. He sniffed the strong smoky aroma of the coffee and that itself gave him the prediction of the big bitterness. Then he sipped the hot strong coffee, it was strong enough to witness the bitterness of a filter coffee and the sweetness of jaggery has touched the top of his senses. At every sip of his coffee and at every instance it spreads over his taste buds, he lips curved in joy and he closed his eyes to witness only the taste of coffee but nothing else around him. By the time he finished his coffee and came out of the trance, the plate was empty, and he had nothing to eat.

"Where are the snacks?" he asked with a surprised expression.

"Hm. You were dreaming in your own world with coffee, and I ate them all", Prashanthi replied.

"Huh! Okay dear", he bent over to kiss her forehead and then she went downstairs.

Bhargav is now looking towards the sky and started to draw the shapes of clouds. He perceived one cloud as a horse, one looked like a big laughing Buddha with round tummy, one formed a doughnut and some others looked in different forms in the line of his perception. And then at this moment, far away in the sky he noticed a white flying object. It is an airplane. To his surprise, he could cleary see the name Air India painted on it even from such a long distance. He could even read the flight number on it. And he is actually surprised to see the giant in red and white engineered creature come near him and witnessed it getting bigger and bigger in sight with every second. He closed his eyes in fear and shielded his face crossing his arms over and cried out loud.

"AAAAARRRGGGGHH!!!!"

But he witnessed someone pulling him at once. Sucking him at once into a black hole. Suddenly he found to be greeted by a gorgeous young lady in red saree, with neatly applied makeup, bold red lip stick on her slim lined lips with matte finish, long sharp nose where a nose stud found to be in the right place, with baby pink blush fairly smeared at cheek bones and hair tightly brushed and tied as a bun. He was stunned by the beauty and has not moved his eye an inch away from her to notice the square cut of her jawbone to the slender long neck and the eyes that could arrest one into a statue and smile that could send a man in whirlwinds.

"Namaste", said the lady.

He too joined his hands and greeted her with a grin, "Namaste".

"Welcome on board to Air India 1265. Sir, please come with me to your seat", she said and guided him through aisle.

A good old English lady with wrinkled face smiled at Bhargav and winked. He looked at her in shock. "Now shut your mouth son", she said. Her daughter just seated beside her who has same facial features as the lady, is in traditional Indian wear, a cotton saree wrapping the pallu around her head. She smiled very gently at him. He followed the air hostess and after two rows of seats one lady looked the pyjamas Bhargav is wearing and cried out a big laugh, "Hahaha... Nice one. It is ducks all over your pyajamas." Bhargav walked past her in bewilderment.

The air hostess walked him through the red carpeted aisle crossing the rows of luxurious red seats with AIR INDIA embroidered on them. He crossed many passengers on board, dressed in different styles. One man introduced himself as Shaktimaan, the first superhero of India. And when Bhargav proceeded to shake hands with him, another one interrupted him, "Hello, I'm the He man, the first superhero of the world." Bhargav shook hands with both of them, one with left and the other with right and passed by them to meet a kid with a scar on his forehead and round eyeglasses with a magic wand in his hand and uttering something to produce a spark and smoke at the tip of the wand. "Hi, I'm Harry from the Hogwarts", he introduced himself.

"I'm Bhargav. It is great to meet you", Bhargav smiled at him.

"Here Sir", the air hostess guided him to his seat. He walked to her and took his seat. Then the air hostess bent over to help him to fasten the seat belt. With her face coming very near to him, he noticed the sweet perfume unrolling from her. This brought a smile on his lips and noticing him the air hostess too smiled back coyly. When she buckled the seat belt and stood up Bhargav looked at name plate pinned to her blouse and a name MALINI engraved in white. "Malini," he read out loud enough to reach her ears.

"Yes sir, I'm Malini. Just reach out to the call button here and we'll be at your service. Do you need anything as of now?"

"No. Nothing", replied Bhargav. Malini smiled and left him to pick up another passenger.

Just in a moment, a lady came in thick red suite and skirt. Her name plate read POOJA SHARMA. "Mr. Bhargav, do you like to have anything to eat or drink?" she asked him. Pooja is a fair skinned lady with athletic type body from Manipur. Her accent almost felt like Russian for him. "Yeah, I would like to have a fresh lime juice", Bhargav asked her pointing with his finger. Then she took a glass of fresh lime juice and stirred it and handed it to him.

Then Pooja asked an English man who is sitting in the same row to the window side, "Sir, would like to have a drink?" Then he folded down The Guardian newspaper and held the cigar that sticking out from his mouth with his left hand and said, "Yes, a medium dry vodka martini, lemon peel. Shaken, not stirred."

"Sure sir, I'll get you the drink", she said and went towards the lockers at the tail end.

Then Bhargav startled to see the James Bond sitting next to him. He just couldn't believe his eyes to see his most favourite hero travelling along with him and that too next to him. Then he exclaimed, "You are!?"

"I'm, Bond, James Bond", he replied.

"Oh! Hi, I'm Bhargav", he is really excited to meet his most favourite hero.

"Oh! It's nice meet you Bhargav", Mr. Bond extended his arm for a warm handshake.

"You're the most favourite hero of mine and I have seen all your movies."

"It's my pleasure Mr. Bhargav. Well, I have pretty good fans in India, and I would really love to shoot some part of my movie here. I love the real, naturistic, and lively locations that are only found here", Mr. Bond's accent of British English filled Bhargav's heart with joy and contentment. Just then Mr. Bond picked up his satellite phone and the screen is flashing with a 'M' on it. James Bond looked at Bhargav like asking for an excuse to take the call and he smiled in acceptance. “Hello M, 007 here”, and he continued his talk with her. But Bhargav from inside wanted to ask if they both really had a romantic relationship and wanted to talk to her.

But he started to notice the chiseled personality of the James Bond. He is slim built with sharp cut jaws clean shaved, short and trimmed hair. He is a perfect fit to the personality as described by the creator Ian Fleming. He wore a nicely tailored mel grey suite with brown checks, thin lined and medium sized checks. The bronze coloured cufflinks made a good match. His white shirt and navy blue tie gave the dynamic look that is always a mandate for the James Bond.

Then in the moment Malini walked along with the new passenger. She is a petite built lady and set the temperatures high in the midair. She has put a gold plated band on her forehead with a star engraved on it that held her lustrous curly hair. She wore bronze armour that had a golden plate cupping over her breasts and a golden belt around the waist that held the thick metallic blue bottom wear. She wore a pair of high knee shoes and carried a lightening whip hanging to her waist. And yes, she is the Wonder Woman.

Bhargav is now astonished to see her on board, that tall figure walking with a charismatic smile. Malini introduced Bhargav to her, “Prince Diana, he is one of our guests on board, Bhargav.” He looked with a wide grin and kept staring at her till there is an announcement from another crew member to fasten the seat belts and get ready for the further journey.

The flight suddenly picked up speed flew over the Himalayas and the flight captain called upon the passengers, “Good evening, ladies and gentlemen. Welcome on board to Air India 1265, Boeing 787 Dreamliner. I'm the flight captain Robin Sharma, the monk who sold his Ferrari to fly this big machine. Now we are flying over the Mt. Everest, the highest peak in the world. And there on, look towards your right side and see the Great Wall of China." The captain flew the flight to London and moved close to the Big Ben to show The Thames and then to Amsterdam to witness the beautiful floral gardens, he flew to the Sahara and crossing the sand dunes and the Pacific, he flew over to the Amazon valley. After flying over Sydney Opera House and among tall buildings of Tokyo, the flight reached the sacred Ganga. Bhargav bowed his head and joined his hands to offer prays at Ganga. The James Bond and Wonder Woman followed same as he did.

Then the flight suddenly went through the turbulence. Everyone held their seats tighter and some of them were screaming out of fear. A lady from the crew made an announcement asking all of them to be seated in their seats and fasten up seat belts. Bhargav shut his eyes again in fear, all the faces he could remember are Prashanti, the James Bond, Prince Diana and sweet Malini. But he shuttered his eyes tighter. Suddenly, he opened his eyes to see the dark sky filled with stars and his wife trying to wake him up.

"Get up Jaanu, how long are you going to sleep?" Prashanti raised her voice louder.

"Huff. Wait dear, Am I asleep till now?" Bhargav is still in his turbulence.

VIII

THE EAGLE AND THE FISHERMAN

Linga was looking towards the serene blue waters that met the skies at the end of the sight and hitting the shore in tides, the same water but different tides. The tides float some tiny crabs to shore and bathed the snails on the rocks every time they hit the sands and the rocks off shore. He is lying down on his belly on a shaft in the fishing boat anchored at bay that swinged restlessly with the restless tides. He didn't know what the time was and could see no fishing boat coming this way. The bright sunrays were scorching him and sweat was dripping, but he waited for his father's boat to arrive with patience.

Meanwhile, some five people arrived there on bikes and parked them on the approach road far away from the shore and walked in the sand lifting their feet heavily. They were laughing loudly making some fun, one among them was walking behind trying to drop off the sand that entered his sandals. They walked to shore to click some photographs posing against the fishing boats ashore. Linga looked at them and sighed, “Huh, these guys are of no use. They come and bargain but don’t buy any”, he spoke to himself.

And from the direction of the village huts Dasaraj called him, "Hey..! Linga, have you seen your father’s boat coming? He promised for a big catch today." Linga turned his head and waved his hand signaling to say a no, “He always wants to bully my father. Such a crap he is”, he spoke to himself again.

Then, after a short while a boat appeared approaching the shore with three people on it. Linga identified his father on it in the front end. A wide grin came over his face, then he stood up and blew a loud whistle to Dasaraj saying that his father has come. Ramappa also found his son waiting for him and waved both of his hands in joy. As the boat came nearer they stopped the motor and glided into the harboring area. And more nearer, all of them got down to push the boat through the shallow waters and the other boats anchored on the shore. Linga jumped off the boat and went to lend his hand. They had to push with great force for the boat to move over the sand and water to reach anchoring point and finally, they stationed it.

Ramappa along with Somayya, his companion on the boat has grounded the heavy fishing net. It had a very few fish than usual and it is not a good catch for the day. Just in the moment some other fishermen gathered around and started to unwind the net and lay it open, and Ramappa is taking out the fish one after the other.

Dasaraj, the head of the fishermen dropped by just to witness Ramappa’s luck and humiliate him. "Ramappa! Do you remember what you have challenged me today? Do you think this small catch would justify your virile words?" Dasaraj laughed louder and the other men also joined him.

Ramappa with his head down, continued to take the fish from the net. Linga burned with rage and gave a ferocious look. But he is a kid and did not know how to counter him with words and kept silent.

"No one is going to be lucky enough every day. There is definitely a day which is called which is called to be mine. And be sure that you would not lose your head post some or the other day", Ramappa replied him to exhibit his valour.

"Huh! Haha.. stop boasting yourself Ramappa. Show some valour in your catch", Darasaj left the place in anger. Dasaraj is always in to show off his luxuries and assets. He goes to every place in white clothes and sunglasses clinging to his ears every time. He grew a big moustache and curled at tips and rides on his black Royal Enfield. It was long time ago, that Dasaraj had a large catch that had a rare fish and a big one too. He made a good fortune that day and he was praised by all the fishermen in Brahmangudi and surrounding villages. That reputation continued for a long time that earned him the head man cadre. It was said that there is no other fishermen till now who is a fitting match to Dasaraj. Since, then Dasaiah became Dasaraj.

"This Dasaraj is going to change into the old Dasaiah again. And those are days are here to come by", Ramappa spoke to his men and continued his work.

Ramappa pulled out all the fish one by one and put them on ground and Linga separated them accordingly. Seeing from a distance the youngsters came to the boat to see if they can buy some fish. The boys found that no variety of fish was caught in sufficient number to make a buy. Somayya suggested them to buy two or three varieties of fish together. They boys were not convinced with the offer and left. Somayya murmured in dissatisfaction and hesitatingly continued to unwind the net and collect the fish.

And just then an eagle hovered over there and flew closely to the catch. And its shadow caught Ramappa's attention and little did knew it's intention of flying closer to the ground. Every other moment it flew closer to the fish, it took a note of them, the number, sizes and suitable ones. Ramappa's suspicion grew every time after seeing it's claws that were ready to pick a piece of his catch. He alerted Linga, "Son, take your catapult. This eagle may steal our fish at any moment. You just keep an eye on it." Linga jumped into the boat to find his catapult and some stones that were kept ready. He found it in the utility box and was getting ready to position himself to safeguard the little catch that would earn the bread for the day.

Then the eagle also worked on its wits. Finding Linga away from the pile of fish, he flew by stretching his wings to flap them more harder to build up his velocity, brought his legs close to the breast, opening claws wider to fit a nice sized fish and with its sharp sight, eyed a nice one to pick. He grew his speed and moved straight towards his aim and Linga alarmed himself and made an attempt to attack. But he lost to the eagle's speed, and it picked up a fish from the catch, flapped his wings more harder and quicker to get away with his catch. Linga flung his head down to convey his futile attempt to his father and his allies.

"It's okay Kanna. Come up here and stay close to us. You should be careful not to be hit by the eagle's sharp claws. Got it", Ramappa patted his shoulders.

Now the eagle started circling over them again. This time not much closer but Ramappa suspected another attack. After circling a few rounds, it flew close to the ground and Linga lifted his catapult aiming the eagle. The all alert eagle skipped Linga's aim and tilted to a side and changed its course of flight. After this rehearsal kind of attacking act, the eagle flew to high skies and hovered over there slowly, like it is a meditating Yogi who found his peace. Ramappa and his companions also relaxed and continued to segregate the catch. Few moments passed and the presence of an eagle is no longer in their thoughts till it's shadow passed over them closely to be able to be noticed. Linga is alert again with catapult in position. But he learned that the mighty eagle played a trick on him. "Relax Kanna, be easy," Ramappa said.

And with no moment's gap, the eagle flew to the ground and picked up a nice fish and escaped from there. Ramappa cried out loud this time, his poor catch of the day, the eagle's attack and Dasaraj's humiliation made him furious and that built up some frustration in him. He sat on the ground looking towards the fish, lifted his eyes towards the sky cursing the eagle and looked towards the waters in dismay.

"Hey Ramappa, now don't just sit like that. Come on, this catch will at least be sufficient for a day's meal. Let's share this among three of us and take home. We'll plan for a nice catch again, this time we shall go for deep sea fishing. Come on, now we shall return home," Ramappa's another man, Masenu spoke. Now they rolled the fishing net neatly, tied it together and laid it in the boat. Meanwhile Linga shared the fish in three equals and kept them in separate baskets. All of them walked to the houses together with casual chit chat.

When the day is coming to an end and when the moon and stars were taking their course of action to delight the sky, the street lights are lit, some eateries showed up with fritters and pakodas, some with fried fish and kebabs grilled on traditional earthen stove. Eventually, some arrack and toddy pots popped up along. The three big men handed the baskets with fish to Linga to deliver them at their houses and asked him to stay home. These men got a call from a corner of the street. It is Kantham, a mid aged, lustrous street vendor who sell some fried fish. Now they bought a bottle of arrack for each and fried fish and sat far away from the crowd to relish the pleasant evening's moon.

They've finished the drink and the alcohol started talking in them. They are yelling at each other, made jokes and talked rubbish. They are lost from the place and mind. After an hour or more, they walked back to their homes.

When Ramappa reached home, he found Linga already asleep and his wife, Jaya winding up some household chores. She was enraged on seeing heavily drunk Ramappa and slammed the door behind them and asked him, "Should you drink even on the day when had the worst catch and you earned no money? What would I buy for house?"

Ramappa had nothing to reply back to her and looked at her in despair, walked out of the house and sat in the porch. Jaya served him food there in the porch with fish curry. After he finished eating he came back and lied down in the porch looking at the sea, the beautiful one in the night and that looked more than beautiful in the moon light. That sound of tides hitting the shores was heard like a white noise zeroing every emotion one had. The cool, serene, calm winds that blew were felt like the angels fanning the children of the sea to sleep. Jaya called Ramappa to come inside and sleep. But there is no reply from him and she found him already asleep. Now Jaya shut the doors slowly not disturb his sleep and bid him a goodnight with smile on her lips and love from her heart. The silence of her spoke here.

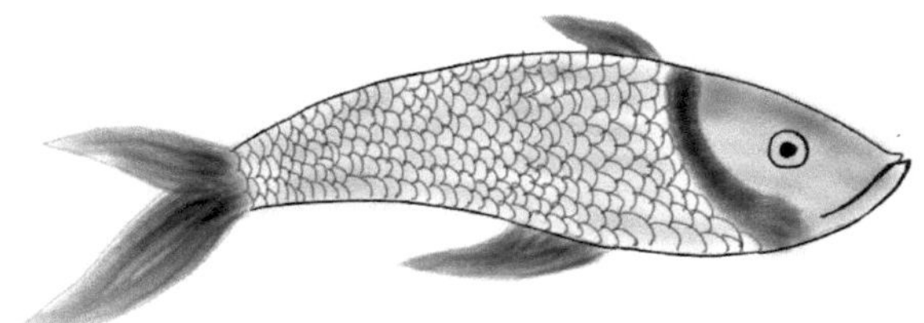

IX

PERFUME AND THE GUTTER

Rajesh delivered a fast ball to Kiran and as he missed it, the ball went past wickets and hit a flower pot behind them. "See, you'll be denied bowling next time, if you bowl fast", Karthik from the bowling team warned Rajesh. "Yeah, it's ok. It went by as a habit."

"I have warned you many times not play inside the compound. You've broken many pots till now and you've hit one more today", Meera aunty warned us from her balcony.

Meanwhile, our wicket keeper Manohar couldn't trace out where the ball has gone amidst the clump of flower pots and bushy plants behind them. So, he called me for help, "Tejas, come here and find the ball."

I quickly moved from my position and helped him to find the ball that was struck in the bushy hedge plants. "Rajesh, here is the ball", I found it and threw it to him.

All the boys positioned themselves once again. Kiran the batsman, Arun as runner, Manohar behind the wickets, always ready to run out the batsman, I'm on the mid off and no fielding on leg side, a hit towards the leg side has no runs and it's an out when the ball goes out of the compound wall directly and it is the batsman's responsibility to get the ball, Karthik took his place as slip, Rajesh the fast bowler on 22 yard pitch, has slowed down for the gully cricket. Ajay and Surya from the batting team seated themselves away from the pitch.

Rajesh delivered another ball to Kiran and he has hit the ball in the gap between Rajesh and me that is hard enough to reach the boundary line. Kiran and Arun tried to take a run and switch their places. I ran fast to catch the ball and threw it back to Rajesh and he was at the wickets to receive and he had almost hit the wickets before Kiran reached the crease. But, Kiran too was quick and saved his wicket.

"Aaargghhh!!" I would have taken your wicket, but you're a lucky fellow.

***

On the other side of the evening Ali Ahmed Khan was working on his sewing machine, stitching a new dress that a customer would collect after this evening's namaz. He is taking a look at the wall clock intermittently, so he has to finish stitching quickly and attend Maghrib on time.

"Ji, I've kept water ready to take bath, towel is on the hanger. Ok?" Ali's wife Nusrat has reminded that it is already time.

"Haan haan, theek hei. Yehi poora karke jayenge", he replied and pedaled his sewing machine a little faster. He was pulling the cloth under the needle at quick pace and with precision not to miss any inch of the dress. The needle was continuously piercing through the cloth carrying a white thread to other side and pulling out after binding a strand of thread from there and stitching the cloth together.

Ali gave a few more stitches and finished the dress. Finally, he lifted the dress that he has tailored with perfection and held it with his raised arms and inspected his work in detail. The white kurta with floral design around the neck embroidered with cobalt blue thread, and buttons with diamond cut glass beads; a slim embroidery design in blue and thick cream colour around the cuffs. Finally, a strip of design at the bottom cut. All the cloth was perfectly tailored to fit a twenty two year old young man.

The time has already clocked 4.20 PM and Ali rushed to take a bath. He washed neatly and assured himself that he is clean enough to enter a Masjid. Now he has killed ten minutes of his time to dress up, comb his hair neatly, to make his beard and mustache fine. He then picked a wooden box that was said to be being used from his great grandfather's time to keep attar, the traditional perfume. It was made of rich dark rose wood, the lid has carvings of flowers in the left bottom corner and to the right top corner a cresent moon and a star were carved along with a verse in Arabic praising the lord. He opened the lid and a great mixture of fragrances filled the air around him. As this brought a bright smile on his lips, he passed fingers over the several bottles of his finest collections and picked a jasmine attar that once he bought from an old merchant on his visit to Kerala.

"Yes, this will be a nice pick for the evening", he spoke to himself and applied a bit of it on his clothes. Now he carefully placed the box in almirah, moved out of the room and called his daughter, "Amina beti, where are you?"

"Haan baba", Amina appeared from kitchen.

"Amina, I'm going for the evening namaz. I've left a new dress on the table, could you please iron that before I return. Our client will come here and pick it up on his way back to home from Masjid", Ali asked his daughter for a help and she gave a nod for it. "Okay baba. But, I'll charge for it."

"Haha, ok beti", he brushed Amina's hair and left for namaz. He once again ensured that he is perfectly tidy and that the perfume was strong enough to be recognized. He put on his topi and adjusted it and seemed to be fit.

He walked on the street with his head slightly lifted, a bright smile on lips and a gentle pride in his eyes. He greeted some of his friends and elders on his way his to the evening prayer.

***

Now it is Manohar's turn to bowl to Kiran. The duo has scored eighteen runs after a battle of the balls and the bats in the last three overs. The 5th Cross on Road no. 2 in Kalyani Nagar is filled with the loud cries of the boys and knocking sound of the bat and ball intermittently.

Ali, who lived on road no. 3 in Kalyani Nagar, has to reach the Masjid in road no. 1 and has to walk through the 5th cross of road no. 2. As Ali walked ahead, he witnessed the row of congested houses on a narrow path and the smell emitting from the gutter irritated him. He covered his nose with a handkerchief and walked looking towards the road.

Kiran is ready at the crease to face Manohar's ball. He took his position and held the bat firmly and tapping it continuously on the ground indicating his readiness. And Manohar at the bowling end has discussed his strategy with fellow team mate and was ready to ball.

Ali walked quickly past the houses 2-67 and 2-66 without lifting head up and covered his nose still uncomfortable with the odour.

Manohar's ball came straight to Kiran's foot and on leg side. So he had to take a back foot and lift the bat to hit it.

Kiran got tempted and hit the ball on th edge of the bat and straight away it went out of the compound. "And it is an outta", Manohar shouted loudly.

Manohar's loud noise caught Ali's attention when he is at 2-65 and lifted his head up and a red colour cricket ball coming from nowhere is in Ali's sight. It straight away fell in the gutter and it spilled some sewage on Ali's white clothes.

"It is the batsman who has to bring the ball now", I pointed to the direction where the ball has gone. And Kiran obeyed the rules of the game and walked out to find a man in white clothes and a topi on his way to evening namaz, who is furious with some dirt on his clothes.

Ali shouted at the boy who came out in search for the ball. He stood there in fear and didn't move an inch. All of a sudden a few more boys came along and witnessed the scene. They apologized and pleaded guilty for what has happened. But Ali is upset for what has happened and that he would be late to the Maghrib. After venting out a few more notes to dispense his anger, Ali left the place and walked back to home to clean and attend the namaz.

***

Amina on the ironing table heard the gates opening and came outside to see who it is. On seeing Ali returning too early, she exclaimed, "Baba, you returned too early! And what is that on your clothes?" Ali told her what has happened on his way to the masjid and walked towards the washroom behind the house. He dumped the clothes in a bucket there and took bath once again.

He entered through the back door from the kitchen side and heard his wife cursing the boys after learning about the incident from Amina. Ali felt bad about his wife blaming the innocent boys and stopped her, "Nusrat, how could you say those words about them. It is an unfortunate incident and they are not intended to do so. Anyhow, they've pleaded guilty and that is enough."

Ali walked into his room silently, took ironed clothes from wardrobe and put them on. He drank some water and left again for namaz. He again took the same route that he has taken earlier in the evening. Now he walked with full awareness and when he turned to the 5th cross on road no. 2, he again covered his nose to avoid smell and kept eyes towards door no. 2-65 and observed the skies to find if any UFO like cricket ball coming towards him again. This time he walked with utmost care, taking a step by step slowly.

Meanwhile, the boys have closed their previous innings and started a new game. Now, I'm on the runner side and Karthik is in the batting crease and ready to hit a ball from Arun. Arun took few steps to come into the action and delivered a spin ball that bounced well to the waist length and Karthik has hit it with energy and into the air, the ball was out the compound wall, "Yay! He is out", one of them from the bowling team cried out loudly.

As Ali reached the spot where he has stopped thirty minutes ago, he heard the boys shouting out of joy and raised his eyes to see that his fears have come true and a ball went flying again, bounced twice on the road and fell straight in to the drainage and spilled the sewage again. It almost fell near him and it is Ali's luck that he missed this time as he took a back foot to safety. Now Ali raged with anger and shouted at the boys and with a high voice.

Inside the compound of Ms. Meera, the joyous cries of the boys suddenly came to a halt after Ali's loud voice filled the place. They were in shock once again and then Karthik slowly opened the gate to find that it is the same man shouting at them again. Ali's body posture itself pictured his anger; he stiffened his arm muscles, clinched his fists strongly and slightly bent forward to gather energy. The boys came out of the gate one after the other and the people in the neighborhood came out into their balconies to witness the evening. Just in time, Raghunath an old man in the locality approached to calm down Ali and spoke to him softly. He then relaxed and spoke to the elder person and narrated the incidents that took place in the evening and how he was hindered from attending the namaz. Ali calmed down after having a dialogue with the Raghunath and temperatures of the situation dropped down. Raghunath scolded the boys so that Ali would not react again on them and sent them away.

And when Ali was to depart from the place, the prayer has already started in the Masjid and it was being heard from speaker arranged on the minar. Ali in despair, looked towards sky, murmured some verses and turned back to return home and the boys have also closed the play and called it a day and returned to their respective homes. So as the birds returned to their nests and called it a day. The darkness emerged from the East skies and the day came to an end when everyone departed to their respective places.

X

AARYA

When the evening skies started to grow darker gradually at snail pace, the atmosphere in the Sundari Nrityalaya on Gariahat road is still peppy with many young girls performing some artistic moves with tapping their feet in unison, swinging and twisting their arms in uniform rhythms and with beautiful expressions on their faces. Sometimes with a smile, a furious face with big round eyes, with a graceful charisma like a Goddess. Yes, the team has been practicing the moves composed by the tutor Sumitra Banerjee to the pitch of perfection, which they're about perform at the commencement of Durga Navaratri celebrations. The air in the dance school is totally filled with the soulful music, sounds of tapping feet in unison and suddenly a loud cry was heard and the practice has come to a halt. The centre position dancer Aarya Ganguly has slipped off and injured left her ankle. All the pupils gathered around and made her sit; it was very painful that she couldn't put any weight on her foot. Ms. Sumitra approached quickly and was shocked to see Aarya's condition. Then she called off the day and asked for

Jayanthi's assistance to take Aarya to a first aid.

****

The clock has struck 8 PM and Mrs. Rachana Ganguly was sitting in the porch and looking at the dim lit street waiting for her daughter Aarya to return home. She is getting restless with every moment the evening is growing into the night's darkness. She could see many vehicles passing by, but Aarya is not seen. Just then Amitav walked out to the porch to find his wife burning with anger and burying herself in fear. He reached to her and laid hands on her shoulder and warmly asked, "What happened? You look so tensed."

"Aarya has not come yet. She lifted my call an hour ago and said she'll be coming soon. But it's getting late."

"Oho! Dear. She'll be safe to home, don't worry. Take things positively, she might be practicing her dance class a little longer, she hardly had three more weeks for her first ever stage performance", Amitav tried to calm her down.

"Of course, she needs a lot of practice. But how long does it take to travel from Ballygunge to Bhowanipur? I'm worried about that", Rachana expressed her fear.

"Yeah, she'll come safe. Okay? Now you come inside", Amitav asked her.

When they're about to move inside, Jayanthi has come to drop Aarya and stopped by the entrance gate, honked and called Rachana to open the gates. She rushed to the gates and opened. Without any second thought she got furious over Aarya and asked, "What took you so long? And where is your scooty?"

"Maa, wait for a minute. Will you let me in?" Aarya replied and Rachana sensed that her daughter is in some pain. And Jayanthi drove her till the porch and when she got off the scooty, Amitav exclaimed, "Oh my! What happened to your foot dear, are you injured?"

"Yes papa."

"How did that happen, have you hit anyone while driving on the roads?" Amitav questioned again in anxiety. Rachana cried out in grief, "Beta, what happened and what is that bandage on your foot?"

Aarya rolled her eyes after being bombarded with a series of questions and Jayanthi answered instead, "Auntie, she slipped off in the practice session and had an ankle sprain. Sumitra ji has taken her to the doctor. The doctor said she'll be fine in two days or three; but had to keep away from practice for few days."

"Oh! Come in beta, I was so much worried that you're not home yet. The day was good, you just had a small injury", Rachana was still worrying about Aarya's condition. They thanked Jayanthi for taking effort to drop her home and bid her a goodbye.

****

After a day's rest at home, Aarya was ready to attend college and could walk slowly for shorter distances. Her ally Jayanthi Biswas picked her in the morning to college. Her only intention was to meet her boyfriend Suman Bhomick and speak her heartful about the later day's incidents. As every other lady, she wished for a solace and a comfy talk from her male counterpart. She had foreseen some love and pep talk. But, little did she expect about the upcoming episode and the events.

Aarya had been waiting for the college hours to finish and meet Suman at cafeteria and her dopamine levels kept rising with every hour foreseeing to meet him. She has sent him several texts during the day but only received some stiff replies. Yet she was excited see him and rushed to cafeteria immediately after finishing the day's college hours. After waiting there alone at a table for some twenty odd minutes, Suman appeared there with few of his friends. Aarya felt embarrassed to wait alone for that long and encountered him with a serious note, "Why did you take so long to come and see me? I had been waiting here for almost twenty minutes."

He looked around to see if anyone was observing them. Two of his friends were watching him, he gave a short smile and turned towards Aarya, "Did you call me here to embarrass me in front of all these guys? Shit, I shouldn't have come just to get insulted by you."

His words shook her and she is now almost in tears. She held back the dripping tears and lowered her face that nobody shall find her crying. Suman took the seat on the other side of the table and said, "Okay, now stop that, I'm sorry."

After a moment of silence, Suman himself started the conversation, "How is your injury now? Do you still have pain?"

"Yes a little. But the doctor asked not to attend dance classes for some days. I may not be able to perform for the navaratri celebrations too", she replied with moist eyes.

Aarya doesn't know what has gotten into Suman or something has possessed him. He has suddenly gone mad at her and made severe insults, "When you cannot dance properly, you should have sit quiet at home. Why do you need all these? I hope you've had enough for now and need not learn any dance or any other circus moves."

After witnessing this awkward behavior, Aarya had no words to speak to continue the conversation. She didn't get what she wanted from him, not at least little respect but an unexpected offence. She is now almost wrecked in grief; tears rolled down her eyes and started sobbing. Suman left the table for Aarya to sob alone. She is deeply hurt and broken with his absurd actions. Jayanthi came by her side immediately to console her and took her away from the place and left for home.

****

Aarya was all alone in her room sitting beside window looking at the deserted street and underestimating her caliber and bringing some pathetic thoughts into her mind. Amitav wondered what his daughter might be doing alone in her room and doesn't want her to buildup any toxic thoughts. So, he took some menthol massage oil from his cupboard, went to see Aarya and greeted her with a wondrous smile that lifted her mood, "Hello beta!"

"Hi baba!"

"What are you in your day dreams? A high rated dancer that won many applause and hearts of her audience!"

"Haha.. Nothing like that baba, I was just watching the road", she replied to her father.

"You should give a positive vibe to your dreams at least and they manifest into reality", he gave her some booster.

"Yeah, I'll dad."

Now he sat by her side and took her foot in his hands to apply some oil. She pulled back, but Amitav said, "It's ok beta, let me give some massage it'll relieve some pain. Do not think any low about yourself, this is not any end, you can still give your best. Do you remember any moment that has triggered the passion towards dance and that inspired you? Of course, I've never asked you about that. I hope you remember, don't you?"

"Yes", she uttered slowly.

The memories of her visit to the Hangseswari Mandir in Bansberia were still afresh in her. It was seven years ago during her high school excursion she visited the shrine that looked more like the Moscow's Pokrovsky Cathedral that caught her vision. But she had a little more to explore there, the Anantha Basudev temple that was adjacent to the Hangseswari shrine. She was unknowingly drawn towards the temple that was built of terracotta and the porous walls that had the glorious sculptures carved on them depicting the beauty of Bengali classical dance the Gaudiya Nritya. She walked along observing the exponentially alluring sculpture of the dance poses that narrate the epics and the musicians who held many instruments from Sitar to the Tabla and Harmonium to the Shehnai. Aarya's enthusiasm grew like never before. She has spent all the day's time in that small temple looking and observing the carvings careful and determining every detail that she could take a note of. Her interest grew much stronger and a passionate determination was made by the young Aarya to learn the classical art. And when she expressed her interest to her parents, they were happy to enroll her in the Sundari Nrityalaya where the genesis of a dancer occurred. And there were a lot of transformations aftermath.

All the experiences for that day have flashed in her memory just in a moment and this has elevated her mood and lightened her heart; Amitav noticed a tiny smirk on her face, "It's ok beta, sleep now. We shall go to a place tomorrow."

"Where?"

"Dakshineshwar."

"Ok baba, sure. Good night", she bid a goodnight to Amitav.

****

All the Sunday morning for Amitav and Rachana went by with regular gardening, visit to a market to buy some vegetables and to finish up all chores that a working mother and father would have. Aarya had to take rest as she could move very little and her sister is the only one who could only help her parents. And after a nice Sunday meal all of them took a little rest and almost when the time is around 3 o'clock four of them got ready to make a move for the short trip as planned.

All of them were seated in the car and Aarya occupied the front seat beside her father to avail enough leg room. They drove for almost one hour through the busy roads from Ballygunge towards Dakshineswar in dense traffic and slim roads to reach their evening's destination. They quickly walked in to the temple premises and entered the queue for the security checks and moved towards the sanctum sanctorum for the deity's darshan. They've entered the high ceiling painted in cream and red colours, the sanctum sanctorum that hosted the Maa Kali. The black and short deity, that appeared beautiful and blessing to whom approached with love. The deity with golden crown and big bright nose ring and decorated with garland of red and yellow flowers. She placed her right foot on a demon and held a head of another demon in left hand. The deity also held a lotus in one hand, a weapon in one and seemed to be blessing with another hand. She was draped in crimson red saree and decorated with lotus and other flowers.

Aarya was very much pleased to see the treaty visual of the Goddess Kali. She closed her eyes to feel the bliss of the mighty Goddess, to know the presence of her strength, love, beauty that was filled in her vicinity. When Aarya closed her eyes, the Goddess Kali's charming glory was the only picture that she could see. The round big bindi with kumkum that was the third eye; the bright eyes that always showered love, her beautiful smile as a symbol of peace that she could instill the lives of her believers; the palms that were smeared with turmeric, seemed to be blessing to whomever approached her to surrender themselves and enlighten; the demon's cut off head and an axe as a symbol that she would kill the ego and the falsehood of the man. As a mother, she has all the elements in her. As an eternal mother is everything on this land. She is the Shakti.

Aarya opened her eyes moistened. Amitav held her by shoulder and walked out of the sanctum sanctorum to the hall way. Four of them walked along and came to a corner of the corridor, where few people gathered and were talking. Most of them in the gathering are youngsters, some adolescents and elder youth. Few older citizens sat leaning against the wall, dressed in white khadi kurta and pajama. Now one amongst the senior citizens there, held a book in his hand and occupied the center place. Now all of them calmed down and positioned themselves properly. Amitav and his family also seated themselves in the small crowd.

The elder person, who was to deliver the discourse, introduced himself to the gathering; clearing his throat, he spoke with deep vibrant voice, "Good evening all. I'm Dhanunjaya Bhattacharya, this evening we shall have a talk about the Maa Kali as she had been praised in the Mahishashura Mardhini stotra, written by Adiguru Sri Sankaracharya. And I'm happy to see many young faces here." When Aarya was already enjoying the bliss, this added more to it. She is going to have a discourse on the song that her crew had been practicing for months to give their performance for the Navaratri.

With a big smile on his face, he started to recite the stotram.

"Ayigiri nandini Nandithamedhini viswa vinodhini nandanute"

Daughter of the Himavantha, whose presence gave joys to the world.

"Girivara vindhya sirodhini vasini", who resides on the peaks of the Vindhya mountains.

"Vishnu vilasini Jishnunute", who delights Lord Vishnu and praised by Indra.

"Bhagavathi hae shiti kantha kutumbini bhuri kutumbini bhurikrite"

Oh mother! The associate of Lord Shiva and the mother of all creations of the universe.

"Jaya jaya hey Mahishasura mardhini, ramyakapardhini sailasuthe"

Hail the mother who destroyed the demon Mahishasura, the mother with beautifully braided hair and elegance, who is the daughter of the mountain Sailendra.

Thus, he continued to recite the stotra and asked the gathering to repeat after him and also he illustrated the beauty of the Goddess, her divinity, her mercy, her anger and different forms of the Goddess. The old man also described her warrior skills, how she destroyed various demons and acts of valour and strength. By the end of his discourse, he filled the place with Devi's aura. He shared the bliss of Durga with everyone present there. This evening's discourse had a deep impact on Aarya, she was listening with all ears and soaked herself with his words.

That night before she slept, Aarya kept reciting the stotra to herself and thinking deep and deep about the meaning what the old man talked about at the evening's discourse. When she was on her bed and getting ready to sleep, she examined her injured leg carefully and it looked like nothing in front of the beautiful dance. The pain felt nothing beside the pleasure being a beautiful performer.

***

The next morning, Aarya woke up with a new energy, zeal and started walking without any support and reached the balcony in her room and stood in the fresh sunlight to take the warmth and she felt that some energy is being induced into her. She stepped aback and made a dance pose that is a part of her performance and continued one after the other like she was possessed in a trance. But she felt a little discomfort and recognized that she could not move her left foot it felt heavy. She looked at her injured ankle that was swollen and turned dark after the injury. Now there is a stubborn look on her face and she walked back inside and applied some pain relieving ointment, and some numbness was felt. She now stood up on her feet and slowly tried to make poses though she felt pain. After few minutes, she relaxed lying on her bed and braced the moments with energy.

That evening Aarya attended her dance classes, but the tutor didn't allow her to practice along with the crew. After few sessions, Aarya was allowed to stand in line and practice along with the crew. With time nearing for the day of their performance, Aarya is nearing her perfection and her injury was forgotten and she is totally ready for the first ever performance.

***

On the first day of Navratri, the sense of festival has spread all over the skies of the City of Joy like the perfume fills a room. It's colourful everywhere, it is all crimson and yellow. All the streets were filled with people in joy and smiles everywhere. Maa Kali's idols were surrounded with devotees and chantings and devotion.

And that evening the backstage of Kala Nritya auditorium was filled with the hustle and bustle of many artists all doing their makeup, arranging the costume and taking the final instructions from their tutors. The busyness is seen all over and buzz like noise with the chattering of various voices. All of them dressed up in classical avatars of Deva and Devis, the tutors in traditional attires, the makeup artists sweating to double up the beauty, some helpers and young junior students to help and assist the performers of the evening. The auditorium is packed with artists and audience and then after few performances, the host made an announcement, "Now, the dancers from the Sundari Nrityalaya are here on the stage to perform Gaudiya Nritya the classical dance of West Bengal for the song Mahishasuramardhini. I wish them all the best and hope you all would love the performance."

All the dancers in dressed in turmeric yellow saree and thick red border and floral design spun in golden yellow. Nicely braided hair spun like a bun, decorated with lilies and cassandra flowers. All the ornaments glittering in the yellow stage light like the fresh waters shine in the morning sun. The tinkling sound of anklets made their presence more evident. A round bindi on the forehead gave elegance to their appearance where each one of them looked like a Goddess. Aarya stood in the second line of troop.

The music commenced with a long haul of conch that sent jitters and strong veena musical began in the tune of the song and the strong notes of the strings gave goose bumps to audience as well. With the start of the act, the stage looked like an abode of Goddesses who leaped onto the earth to celebrate the navaratri. All the girls flickered like gold with bright ornaments which caught the eyes of the audience stuck to the performance and the jiggles of the anklets in unison with a rhythm locked their ears. The girls steadily grew their energy with every minute of the act.

Rachana and Amitav Ganguly were in bliss of the moment to witness their daughter's first ever performance and also noticed her pain from the injury. But with a brave determination Aarya still hit the floor firmly and kept her flow with the team. When the performance ended Aarya was able support all her weight only one leg and she trembled with pain. The team stood still after eight minutes of powered act and the crowd seated in the audience stood for a standing appraisal to the young girls.

A shiver on Aarya's lips and teary red eyes with tears dripping on to her cheeks smeared the eye liner. Noticeably with a smile she expressed her victory over a submissive time and also the injury left her immovable for a moment.

XI
TORA TORA

Nandini was eagerly waiting for the long bell to ring and the school hours to be finished quickly than any other day. The only thought of her grandparents at home with whom, she would visit the annual amusement park in the evening, has some space in her boundaries that is to be perceived by her. The grammar that her English teacher teaches is nowhere entering her mind. The ears are involuntarily functioning to sense the sound waves that vibrate the ear drums. The lectures of the physics teacher are totally illogical for her till the swings of toy train swirl her in rounds. The combinations of the chemistry are impractical enough in front of the pink cotton candy. The curve of her elegant smile on the lips can never be perfectly drawn in the geometry and no algorithms were designed to calculate her levels of joy. When the time to say the end of the day has come, she is almost ready with her backpack to rush away after the long bell.

TRRRRRIIIIIINNNNNNGGGG!!!!!

With the ring of the long bell, all the pupils in the school stood in their own places for the national anthem and later with the loud cry of "Jai Hind", all of them were ready to move away and buzzy noise has immersed the corridors and alleys in the school. But bound to the orders of their new principal, the pupils should be sent out class wise from lower to higher and Nandini must wait till the fifth grade are allowed. Just a few minutes of waiting left her impatient and she worried that it would delay her evening. When it was time for them to leave, she rushed like a meteor falling from space to the earth. She cycled with that meteoric speed on roads till she reached home. And leaving her shoes and backpack aside she looked out for her grandfather in his room, on terrace and finally found him somewhere in the corner of the garden piling up the dry fallen leaves and her grandmother assisting him.

"Grandpa. Grandpa.! What are you doing here?" Breathing heavily, she spoke again, "aren't we going to the exhibition fair?"

"Yes darling, we're going."

"Then, why are you here? Get ready," she was breathing like she hasn't got some air for a long time.

"Ayyohh!" Her grandmother sighed and spoke, "why is this girl so fretful, just like her mother," and both laughed in unison.

"It is not time yet, you first freshen up yourself, relax and have some snacks. We'll leave at 6 P.M. Ok!" Nandini sighed at her grandfather's statement and left the garden and ran into house to find if her brother is back from school. There she found him leaning very low in the couch and watching the cartoon show and seemed not to care about the evening's plan of visiting the amusement fair. She walked to him blocking his sight to the T.V. and questioned, "Varun, are you coming to the amusement fair today?"

"Get aside, let me watch this cartoon", his reply is far away to please her in any way. She felt he is too lousy and walked quickly to her mom in kitchen. Just and when Nandini walked into the kitchen she is ready with a glass of milk, stirring some sugar and tapped the spoon on the rim of the tumbler to put the last few drops of milk into it and handed it to Nandini, "Nandu, have some milk and change your clothes."

"You're coming with us to the amusement fair, aren't you?" Her question was straight.

"Yes, we're going. Take a nice bath and relax, we'll leave when your father is back to home. Okay!" Nandini's smiley lips covered with a white milk moustache.

She then sped away to take bath and was ready to leave at any moment when others are also ready. She wore a simple light rose pink frock with beaded design on chest and lavender coloured waist ribbon and down from where big frills gave an incredible look. She took a seat in the living room watching T.V. and likewise hurling everyone to get ready to leave to the fair.

All the six members of the family took a fifteen minute walk to reach the public grounds that was almost a kilometer away. All along the walk Nandini held her grandfather's hands, she walked joyously talking to her grandparents, jumping, and dancing and always kept herself away from her father's eyes.

At the entrance gate of the fair, two huge mascots stood on the either side welcoming all the visitors of the evening and Nandini thinking of them that they really are same, smiled at them widely and waved her hand calling them, "Hi!". They waved back in return, which made her feel like if she was floating on the clouds and light. The premises of the fair, right away from the entrance was lit with electric lamps and LEDs, many people walking in and out with dust rising high, the ground lined with stalls exhibiting their items and welcoming the visitors and a part of the ground spared for the amusement games.

Just at the entry point, there is a board lit with red bulbs "ROBOT HOROSCOPE". Nandini hanging to her grandpa's arm asked if she could go there. And hearing an objection from Nandini's father, her grandpa intervened, "It's alright Kishore. I'll take her."

The stall was totally lit with red bulbs and two robots in red colour suite like Marvel comics Ironman, stood there with screen in the front that has buttons to click and enter the birth date. Nandini stood in front of the robot on a raised platform and a boy handed her a pair of headphones to put on and he turned it on. Soon the facial part lit with small LED lights and the LED screen in the place of eyes blinked 'WELCOME'. Then the boy asked her to enter her date of birth, she carefully typed 31-05-1993. The robot's voice was heard in a male tone, "Welcome". All the light strips on the robot's body lighted up, all along the length of the arms and legs, around the waist and fingers and chest. The robot continued reading out its predictions.

Nandini is holding the headphones over her ears with both the hands, and she playfully looked at her grandpa and fearfully looked at her father. Just then she had seen a family of around eight members enter the premises and a young boy about the same age as her looked straight into her eyes and he started pleading his mother that he too would like to listen the robot horoscope. But she pulled him saying not to waste money on something like that. The voice of the robot barred Nandini to hear what that lady said to her son, but she felt the empathy for the kid. Then after a couple of minutes, the robot finished the saying and thanked. Her grandpa handed the boy a Rs. 10 and they walked away towards other stalls with many toys, handicrafts and food stalls.

There in the open, there were the actual amusement items, the giant wheel; a columbus, that swinged on a rail from one to end to another almost going perpendicular to the ground and the sky at a time and there is another ride, Tora-Tora where a round platform with seats is lifted upon a hydraulic axis and rotated like a tumbling saucer pan. Alongside there are small toy train rides and other. Nandini asked her brother about a giant wheel ride, he involuntarily stammered, “No. No. We’ll go for another one.”

“Hmm. Huff”, she sighed at him remembering the menace he made at the last fair on the giant wheel. That round wheel with series of cabins and totally lighted up with tube lights and some colourful lights. Nandini hoped one could see the full city in a night view when the cabin reaches the top. And that rumbling and pulling session in stomach what everyone would describe, that’s what sounded fun to her. She was only left to see many visitors going around in the giant wheel with loud cries of joy and some of them screaming frightened.

Then she spotted her hand towards Columbus and Tora-Tora, but her father’s sharp looks answered her, and she kept calm. Varun got a nod for Tora – Tora ride and Nandini was asked to satisfy only with a toy train ride. Varun though gave in for a dangerous ride, his knees trembled and Nandini suspected that she has got to witness another menace that he would do again. She felt like her elders are judging her courage and bravery they had never witnessed. After repeated pleading her grandfather recommended that she would go along with Varun for the ride. He put away her father’s objection and obliged his hindrance.

Both the kids grabbed their tickets and the gates. Despite a remarkable wide grin on Nandini's face, Varun prejudiced that she would panic and will not be allowed to alight once the ride begins. "So, you're trying to frighten me?" He warned her, "If you want to leave, just go back now." Nandini not even gave note to him and walked forward.

Soon, they occupied two seats on the inverted saucer pan like platform. When all the seats are filled, the machine underneath made some noise and the platform rotated slowly and was lifted in the air almost to eight feet high. The platform was then tilted to one side and rotation continued. One side of the platform is tilted every time and the other side is lifted sloppy into the air. Varun started to scream, "Ohho ho ohw.." But Nandini was laughing loud and screaming to exhibit her delight, her brother was in a state of shock and her father was startled to her enjoying the ride.

After ride that has put the brother and sister to the extreme ends of an emotion, Nandini walked like she has won a great deal of the evening. She ran quickly to her grandfather, hugged him, and thanked for convincing her father.

Now all the six of them walked to the other stalls and bought some show pieces for decoration. Nandini bought a cotton candy and walked around with her grandpa and played some games and bought some toys. Varun walked with his father's arm around his shoulders. While the two ladies of the house, went around the stalls to buy some coir door mats from Kerala; door curtains, blankets from Hindi speaking ladies; slicers and vegetable peelers and others.

All the last rows of the stalls were food stalls packed with many people, some mobbing around a food vendor, some in queues waiting for their turns, some sitting aside on chairs munching their food and some walking around to find a right one for them. The food bay was filled with aromas of spices mingling around, flavours of various cuisines from around many places of the country. The visuals of vapours from a dosa pan, the smokey smell of frying chicken and noodles from another. Clinking of plates on one side; popping up of the corn on the other and noises of opening soda cans somewhere else. All of these made the visitors' mouth water.

Nandini's father led them to a stall, the board there reads 'Mumbai ka Giant Papad'. That place is filled with many papads fried and some frying in big pans. There, the small raw papad suddenly fries into a big one when dipped in oil and the vendor sprinkled some hot pepper powder and spices onto it before serving. The family ordered one for each of them and Nandini mumbled in her brother's ears, "You've got to taste giant papad, instead of a ride on the giant wheel." Varun least cared her taunting and devoured his snack, she also continued tear large papad stuffed her mouth.

Then on the other side of the stall, Nandini had seen the kid who at the entrance asked his mother for the Robot Horoscope and wasn't allowed to. His big eyes, short hair and innocent looks caught her attention. Holding his mother's hands, he is waiting for his chunk of papad to be handed over. Just then somebody gave a jerk to Nandini from behind and a piece of her papad fell to the ground. This was seen by her father and that serious looks that she got from him, freezed her. Helpless now, she lowered her head to eat rest of the papad carefully not letting any tiny bit of it fall apart.

All the family walked back to home, Nandini still clinging to her grandpa's arms who showered his love on the lovely child of the house.

XII

PIGEONS THAT FLEW AWAY

The inbuilt biological clock for Sam has attended its usual task to wake him early despite his subconscious mind calling from within that it is a Sunday morning. He woke up to know that the time is 5 o'clock in the morning. He involuntarily walked to the washroom to pee and walked back to his room. Living in the same hostel for two years has taught his legs to walk the routes to anywhere in the building.

Sitting on his bed, Sam looked out of the window moving his eyeballs up and down to see the slowly brightening sky and dark floor of the terrace above the dining hall adjacent to the hostel block and continuous with the corridor of first floor. There is a pair of pigeons mingling around flying from the parapet to the floor and back again, bobbing their heads to look around.

Sam was triggered by something, and he quickly slipped out of his bed, and headed towards Kamal's room to take some raw rice that they brought to cook on any leisure evening. He took some grains in his hand and got back to the terrace. The pigeons flew on seeing Sam moving quickly towards them; he halted all of a sudden, now carefully took a few steps forward and scattered the rice grains on the floor. Now he is back at his window to see if the pigeons will come back again to feed on them. But just in five minutes Sam got carried away with some work, his friends who came to see him, distracted him and when it is time for breakfast, he looked at the terrace in a quick blink and walked away. Later, after an hour or two he again went to the terrace and the grains were not found. A faint smile on his face and lighter moment that none of them around there noticed. He lifted his head towards the shiny winter sun and looked around see if there is anyone to ask him what he is looking for. "Hmm. Seems like nobody has noticed me here", he spoke to himself and walked back to his room; switched on his laptop and played some movie to be lost with the time.

On the same evening, Sam along with his friends went to nearby Chanda Nagar Square from tea and smoke. On their way back, he stopped by at a general store and bought half kilo whole wheat. Kamal gave him a questioning look and asked, "What are you going to do with them? Should we grind to flour and make rotis? Aren't Kishanlal's rotis in hostel kitchen enough for our diet?"

"No, these are for some other purpose", Sam's answer was not satisfactory to Kamal. He snatched the packet from Sam's hands and examined them for quality check.

"These are low quality wheat. What will you do with these?" Kamal's question has become an obligation to him. Sam felt that he would be judged and made fun if he reveals that to feed pigeons is his purpose to purchase them. He suddenly turned insecure at Kamal's behaviour and gave no reply in return.

****

Sam woke up early as everyday at 5 A.M. and looked out from his window; no pigeons anywhere and not any other bird. The thought rolled in his mind was 'Maybe they were here yesterday by mistake or by chance. It's good that I didn't tell Kamal why I bought the wheat.' When he was walking back from washroom, he went to the terrace adjoining the corridor and looked around. There is no sign of any bird, but again he felt there is chance that they would come by as they've fed the grains yesterday and look for some today. He immediately brought some handful of wheat grains and threw them on the terrace and stood there for some time, but little away. A bird flew there after few minutes and started to feed on the grains and again few minutes later two more joined it. Sam smiled, his face lit up with glow, he wanted to get some more grains to feed them and moved a little. Noticing Sam's slightest movement, the pigeons feared and flew away one after the other. Sam stopped to move and understood they were frightened. He blew a heavy breath releasing the heavy lungs and walked back to his room.

A few minutes into his book, Sam totally forgot about the pigeons. He noticed the time is already 8.20 and went to take a bath, readied for breakfast, called Kamal and others to dining, and when he is about to leave to the college, he looked towards the terrace noticed that no grain was left over. Now he understood that they would come back again tomorrow, and they will take time to habituate to him.

****

The next morning, Sam brought more grains than the later day; scattered few on the floor and kept some with him as reserve. The pigeons came and started picking the grains and the number increased by one. When the grains on the floor are about to be finished, he turned a little take the rest and throw them. Yet again the pigeons flew noticing his movements, but not too far this time. This brought some confidence to Sam and threw some grains and kept few with him. They came back to the same place to feed and every time he moved his hand to throw grains, or he walked a little, the pigeons flew a little and were coming back to pick the grains again.

This continued for few days, the number of pigeons increased every day, they got habituated to him. Now they don't move or fly away even though he walked among them or threw some grains on the floor. This has become a daily routine during 5 A.M. to 6 A.M. to him. Some days the pigeons would wait there for Sam to give some wheat or any other grains to feed. Now he also kept a bowl of water for them. Many of the hostelers noticed it and few used to look from their widows or from the balconies and corridors. Every time a new person passed through that way, the pigeons used to fly away and return. After few more days, people stopped passing through except the sanitation workers in the hostel.

One morning when Sam was with pigeons feeding them some millets that day, Dev called him from the top of the building, "Bhai, feeding these pigeons is of no use. Better feed your professors what they need. You'd score some good marks in internals."

Sam smiled at his comments, "That is not for my kind of a person. I would feed these birds or some animals just for my happiness, but score grades with my own calibre." Dev smiled in returned, conveying a thought 'This poor guy'. Sam took out his phone from pocket and turned the camera to focus the pigeons along with him in the frame and clicked a selfie. From the adjacent block, Praveen called him, "Sam. Sam.!"

"Yeah, Praveen".

"Kya bhai, ye kabuthar roj aathe yeha?" Praveen questioned.

"Haan, aathe hei".

"Acha! Bahut acha kaam kar rahe ho bhai tum".

"Haha, thankyou Praveen", Sam smiled pleasantly, threw the remaining grains and returned to his room.

That same day, Sam had an argument with a professor over research activities and came back to hostel in the middle of the day. He immediately decided to take a break and prepared to go home for few days, and checked vacancy on the next available train. There are few seats left for a train routing from Kolkata to Hyderabad which would depart in few hours. Booking a ticket and leaving hostel happened in no matter time. He called Kamal to inform his departure after boarding the train.

****

His sudden vacation has happened to extend for a week. Leaving all the work aside and to relax at home was really easy for him. To find a new bird lover for the pigeons has also been easy for them. After reaching home, Sam entrusted the job to feed those birds to Madan, one of his hostel mates. Madan is a humanitarian and Sam believed he would definitely take care of them. But then the things were not as expected and Madan had to stay awake for long nights to finish up his work and woke up late in the mornings, and somebody else started taking care of them. Every morning by the time he reached the terrace over the dining hall, he couldn't find any pigeon there. One evening when he was talking to Sam over phone, he had informed the same.

After week long vacation, when Sam returned to hostel by 4 A.M. on a Monday morning, after a nice relaxing period, he brought a cup full of grains at usual time when he used to feed the pigeons. But there were none of them. Instead he found the pigeons flying on and off the parapet of the terrace of the adjacent block from where once Praveen inquired him about the pigeons. And slowly a dark figure emerged from there and with sun also rising from the same direction, Sam couldn't recognise who it is with daylight hitting from behind.

Then a voice from there spoke, "Bhai, you took a weeklong vacation suddenly, there was no one to feed these poor birds. Then I've taken the responsibility, now they're coming to me", Praveen on the other side explained how he took the lead and laughed. Sam smiled in return and scattered the grains that he brought with him to see if they would come to eat and returned to his room and started working on his research from where he has left it a week ago. And never made an attempt to feed them again, but a last photograph with the pigeons remained a memory.

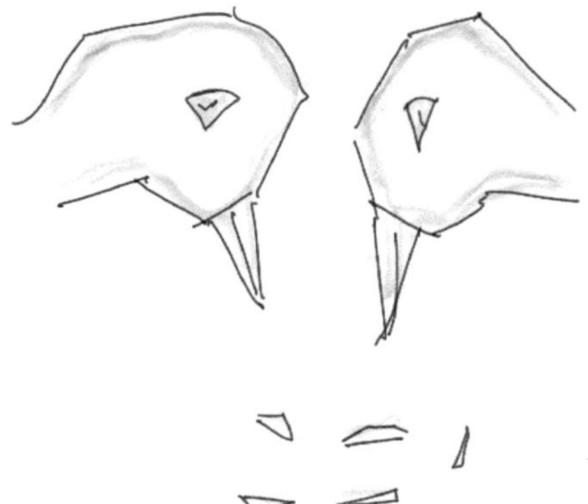

XIII

THE BIG BANYAN TREE

Harsha!"

Harsha!"

Hearing mom call me, I ran through the hall way which was wide, with long pillars along the path that were standing tall under the high terracotta roof and extended space behind the pillars was filled with freshly harvested paddy stacked in gunnies. I stopped by to breath in the strong musk fragrance to fill my lungs and nostrils, and hurried to the backyard and mom was scraping the fish scales and chopping it for dinner tonight. I hugged a pillar in the veranda and leaned to right side and asked her, "Mom, what are you doing?"

"Your father brought a fish for dinner tonight. Go, get some crystal salt and chilli powder from kitchen", with her orders, I paced quickly to the kitchen and returned with a porcelain pot in one hand and a steel container. I'd put some salt and chilli powder in a small plate following her instruction.

"Now put them back in kitchen and play with your friends for some time, I'll prepare dinner", she smiled gently at me. But I returned from kitchen to the backyard and clinging to another pillar now, inquired about brother, "Mom, where did brother go?"

"Yes, Santosh went out to play with his friends."

"Where?"

"No details."

"Hmm", I sighed and left the place, and joined my friends to play. Almost after an hour's play, all of us are sitting on veranda at Nagendar's house; then I saw father dressed in white dhoti and a shirt returning back from farm with a container of milk, I sped away to greet him and walked along with him in to the house. Santosh is already in the home by that time and I've inquired where he has gone to play in the evening, "Where did you go to play in the evening? I haven't seen you anywhere around here."

"I went to play at the banks of Sivahara canal", the village Ramarajapuram has a big canal passing by it, a subsidiary of the river Kameswari which is considered a lifeline to the state and this canal in the delta is a boon to the region. The village on the other side of the bank is Vishwarajapuram. The land connection between the two villages is like a large hairpin loop and four more villages along. All the people from these villages go to Vishawarajapuram to avail any transport and reach the nearby town. Santosh gave more details of where exactly he spent that evening along with his friends, "Did you ever see a big banyan tree there? That is just away from the temple, we were at the tree."

"Whoa! The banyan tree!" I exclaimed in amazement and the reaction from both mother and father was just different. Mother bewildered on hearing that and father was straight away anger.

"How do you think that you can boys can go to that tree? Don't you know that it is not safe and we have heard about the spirits wandering there many times", mom was furious and yelled at Santosh. Father also equivocated with mother to bombard him with questions on who provoked the boys to go there. I was not in any state to understand what was happening in the house, couldn't understand our parents' displeasure, but just kept looking at them yelling at brother with raised eyebrows and wide open eyes.

Later, we were instructed to have a quick bath and all of them had the supper in silence. Father finished food in his plate and walked away to wash his hands, mother waited till father finish and she picked his plate along with her's and walked towards the well to wash them, and before leaving the dining she asked the us to eat quickly. Santosh was drawing figures in his plate in unfinished rice and was looking dumb and sulked. He quietly stood up from there and threw away the leftover rice in plate without anyone noticing it. Then at last, I finished the food and carried my plate, and handed over it to mother to wash. I washed my hands there itself and wiped with my hands dry to mom's saree end and then I stood leaning against a pillar in the veranda. Mom was washing the dishes in semi darkness and in utter silence and peace. I wanted to ask her why she and father were furious about Santosh going to the banyan tree, but I wasn't ready for another round of ferocious drama and quietly walked away from there.

I passed through the hall way and stopped once again to breath in the musk odour of the fresh paddy grain in the gunnies and went back to my room hopping and jumping with some unseen energy. There in the room dim lit with incandescent bulb, Santosh was sitting in a corner on his straw mat and scribbling on a paper, it is a banyan tree. Santosh is a kind of fearless boy with a fascination towards art. I silently stood beside him in a half bent position and hands on my knees and asked, "Does the banyan tree look alike as you drew on the paper?"

Santosh laughed to my innocence and replied without looking at me, "No, it doesn't look like this and your brother is not that great artist to sketch same as it looks."

"And, mother and father were not in a good mood to know that you went to the banyan tree. Is it not good to go near a banyan tree?" I asked him another question.

Santosh was happy for what I was asking rather than how mother and father were furious just an hour ago. He then left the piece of drawing aside turned towards me and began, "You know there is a Great Banyan tree in the city of Calcutta it is spread over 3.5 acres almost in the middle of the city. It is just smaller than our farm land, and many people visit daily. The tree is very old that nobody can find the mother trunk of it. There are few other big banyan trees like, Thimmama Marri Manu in Ananthapur, Pillalamarri in Mahabubnagar, Dodda Allada Mara near Bengaluru and many. They are famous for being old and gigantic, and many tourist visit them daily. And see nothing happens to them."

"How did you know all these?"

"Our teacher in science class taught us, and she has told many things about banyan trees", Santosh replied.

"But why did mother and father ask you not to go there again?" I popped another question to him.

"Huh!" Santosh sighed and continued, "They believe that there is a spirit of a dead man on the banyan tree and they usually say that devils and spirits reside on banyan trees."

"Really?" I was in bewilderment.

"No, our teacher also said these all are myths and superstitious believes of people. Now see, I was at the banyan tree in the evening did anything happen to me?" he spoke like a confident and wise man.

I walked away from him and spread my straw mat on the floor, a blanket and a pillow on it. I pulled myself to the corner and curled up, but out of curiosity I asked Santosh a few more questions. "How big is the banyan tree in our village? Is that as large as our farm land like you said about the other banyan trees?"

"It is not that huge", he continued his work with paper and pencil.

"Will you take me there? I'll not tell anything about this to mother", Santosh startled a little at my advances, turned towards me giving a nod that he'll take me the next day.

The next evening, I was waiting on the temple street near Murthy's Kirana store and Santosh came along with three of his friends. I stood up from there adjusting my rucksack on shoulder and dusted the sand stuck to my pants. Santosh stopped by Murthy's Kirana to buy a snack, after looking through different bottles kept on the counter, he took a sweet candy and asked if I like it. Eventually, I took it from his hands and Santosh paid for the candies and all of us walked away towards the canal road that leads to the place of banyan tree.

The canal road is bit dusty, it is less used and lacks maintenance. Only few elderly people and village youth would go there to spend their leisure evenings. Dhobis wash the clothes and cattle are often bathed there in the downstream. The banyan tree is at the end of the road and people rarely go there fearing about the residing spirits, as a myth being believed for ages.

We were walking along and I asked Santosh why the villagers believe that spirits reside on the banyan tree. And Santosh retold the story that an old pauper once told him about the lady who hanged herself to the tree and how her whole family were dead later. The old pauper also told Santosh that many people say that they experienced a typical wind current blowing there and cries of a weeping woman were heard at night. As we were approaching the banyan tree, a hard wind current blew against them and one of us in the gang feared and fell to the ground. All of us, except Santosh froze in fear and he held his hand to lift him up and said, "Once a young man of the village stayed here for a whole night and disproved the people about any spirits", the boy stood back on feet and Santosh continued, "but the people still believe, and it is a myth my friend. Walk along."

As the banyan tree appeared in front of us, I slowed my footsteps, widened my eyes and a big smile leaped on to my face looking at the lush green tree, the big banyan tree standing on the banks of the canal; the road was cut off at a distance and the water on the other side flows at a distance that it could hardly reach the tree. The big stout trunk as if some ten fat men can fit into it, wide spread branches like an angel stretched her arms, greenish leaves grown thick over the tree like a huge open umbrella and the aerial roots out grown from the branches touching the ground like the rain out pouring through the umbrella. The boys walked to the tree and I first touched the pale pink fresh aerial roots and walked around the tree trying to measure how big it is. Two others started clinging to the roots and swung and teased each other, and the other ran around the tree playfully. Santosh meanwhile, tied two big roots together and called me to sit and swing on them. I walked doubtfully as it was too high and thinking what if I fall from there. Unspoken about the doubts growing in my mind, I walked towards Santosh and he asked, "Are you okay? Will you swing?" I nodded trying to believe him and I was lifted up and made to sit in there to swing, I gripped the big roots tightly. Soon the swing picked up the speed, it was amazing and I chuckled, and consciously not losing grip. After few minutes Santosh ordered me to jump down from there, and I doubtfully looked around and gripped tighter, stretching my legs down to reduce the touchdown impact and took a gentle leap and I was on ground on fours. I played for some time in the sand and swung to hanging roots of the tree and the evening was memorable and that has busted the myths for me.

This had continued for many days till we were abstained from going there when father came to know about our visits from Murthy. A scene of another drama on one evening and both of us tried not to bother them about this and remained calm.

But one day has arrived, when all the family had to go to the big banyan tree one morning except father, whose corpse was already hanging to the tree by his neck. The unending debts and rocketing interests to pay had forced him to part from the family abandoning us in unending grief. The costlier the farming has become, the higher his debts rose. The higher the debts rose and the repayments were delayed and the circumstances lead to his forceful death. He never mentioned about the growing debts and interests that were compounding year on year. The fear and agony has also compounded in him. He once spoke about mounting pressure from the lenders and the death demon has also mounted on his shoulders, forcing him to orphan his family.

Mom was left with no other option but to sell our only possession, the farm we had. The lenders forced her to sell it and our family members could only help them to get better deal for the transaction. Heartbroken by her husband's death, mom decided to migrate with us and moved to her paternal home.

Now the villagers spoke that his spirit would live on the tree hereon.

XIV
THE GREAT BANYAN TREE

"Harsha!"

I was standing still at the banyan tree for so long that I've not known the time. A loud cry from the crowd waiting at the temple has interrupted my thoughts. Deepak Chaddha, my colleague waving his hand to call me back as the Joint Collector is about to arrive soon and a meeting with the villagers and the village headmen is just about to begin.

I travelled eighteen years back still recalling the days I spent in this village and the day the whole village found my father hanging dead to the same banyan tree where I was standing now. The same banyan tree has become a table issue now, which has brought me back to this place.

Just then in no time few vehicles came by and stopped near the temple, and that lifted a faint cloud of dust and sand. A man in white clothes, with a red strap across from his shoulder to waist like the contestant in the beauty contests wear, got down from the SUV with a red beacon on its head. He waited for few seconds, no one knows why and then opened the door. Now a lady stepped out from the car and her appearance, sharp assertive looks reveal that she is an IAS officer and the Joint Collector who was about to attend the meeting.

I whispered in Deepak's ears, "Did you look at her? Nice and young woman, I'm sure she is not married yet."

Deepak bit into my ears, "Dude quiet, anyone may overhear us. You'll be in a trouble."

"Eh!", I murmured and kept looking at her walking into the temple premises only after removing her footwear and she insisted all her staff to remove the footwear and then enter the temple premises. "Whoa! Such a good lady, she follows the cultural norms". Deepak mumbled something again into my ears conveying his intention to stop talking and stalking at the IAS. I okayed with him and noticed that IAS was looking in our direction and I had to adjusted myself to look dignified.

As soon the Joint Collector walked to the dais trailed by some officers and her assistants, all the people summoned at the meeting stood from their chairs and the village heads joined their hands greeting her, "Namaste". She too greeted them in return and all the attendees settled down after a little buzz.

One man introduced himself as Mr. Jogayya, Sarpanch of the village Ramarajapuram and he introduced other important village heads, and all the officers there introduced themselves to the JC. Then Deepak came forward and spoke to her, "Good morning madam, I'm Deepak Chaddha, Site Engineer", and he introduced me to avoid from me spitting out any nonsense, "He is Harshavardhan, Site In-charge and newly appointed architect. We are from the Dhanashri constructions Pvt. Ltd. Thankyou madam." She nodded a little, once at a time to everyone.

Then the village sarpanch turned towards the villagers assembled there and spoke to them, "It is our good fortune that the Hon'ble Joint Collector Ms. Rupali Sharma visited our village today to hear our appeals and any objections pertaining to the newly sanctioned bridge that was to be constructed across the river canal that is passing through the village."

Very soon few villagers and the headmen came forward to put forth their grievances of how they had been facing the difficulties of mobility and transportation from generations. A young man first explained that they have to travel through four hamlets and twelve kilometres to reach the town and this bridge of about half a kilometre would cut down the distance, time and money. A farmer complained about expenses incurred to transport his produce, children complained about taking long walks and journeys to reach a high school nearby and everything as every remote village devoid of a transport means would complain.

"Now that a new bridge was sanctioned, why are some other parties filing objections against that?" Ms. Sharma's question has answer from the people who live on the other side of the bank.

A group of people suddenly rose from their places making loud cries and their arguments were countered by another group. They were not in mood to calm down until a police constable banged on a table to distract the crowd and hit his lathi on the ground. Then one of the local officials said that one of them could be allowed put forth their arguments. Then an old man among them took the lead to speak, he stood up from the chair with help of a walking stick, "Good morning madam, I'm Ramakrishna Murthy, headman of Viswarajapuram, the village on the other side of the canal." He then looked towards the canal and pointing his left index finger to the proposed site of bridge and continued, "The plan of the bridge first proposed has no opposition from our side, but it was objected in this village refusing to uproot the banyan tree here. And in the next plan, the bridge landing at our village is just near to the irrigation canal that acts like an artery to the heart and the construction would lead to cracks to the culvert guarding the canal. And what cost should we nod for the plan," the old man with a depressing frown ended his short note.

Then the Ms. Sharma called upon the engineer from the Public Works Department to ask for what alternative plans does he have. All he could say is that construction at these two chosen points is only feasible and cost effective and safe for the traffic movement. Then she asked him to take her to the proposed construction site. Deepak and I were just watching all the discussion till then and, we followed them to the site and people mobbed around there.

After few moments of pause, she asked for the blue print of the design and when she wanted to speak to the architect of the bridge and we appeared in front of her. "What do you have to say for this design? Can you put forth any solution?"

"Yeah, this plan was designed by the engineer who was previously appointed for the project. I can surely provide a better solution", taking a pause from my conversation I pulled out some big papers from my kit and ordered Deepak to hold them. The clever I carried the surveyed map of the canal that actually showed the shallow points like a terrain map. I continued by pointing my finger at a place on the map, "Here, this is the point where we're standing now and the nearest place to land bridge from here will be this", I showed the narrowest part of the canal with a pointer on the map and briefed her how the new design would not hurdle the downstream flow but the speed riders on the bridge can be.

After a brief discussion for few minutes and she entrusted us a job to prepare a detailed plan, "Hmm. Okay, you can prepare a DPR and present it for further proceedings," she sounded quite impressive, "and where did you get this map of canal, it seems to be very old", her query got a reply from one of my old friends there. "He has taken it from the old panchayat office. Of course, he belonged to this village and lived here eighteen years ago", he walked towards me and held my shoulder firmly.

"Oh! That's great to hear", she exclaimed and smiled for the first time in the day. That simple serene smile revealed her perfectly lined teeth has sent some jitters oh joy to me.

That evening Deepak and I were sitting on the sands of Sivahara canal along with some of my old friends and were munching on some fritters. The smooth flow of waters here hasn't changed any in these years, the gusty winds carried the aroma of soil meeting the waters has enhanced with time and the nights in the village have become more beautiful with beaming street lights, unpolluted air and seemingly beautiful the great banyan tree.

Although indulged in deep conversations with the group, my eyes always caught the sight of the banyan tree that has grown taller and wider in all these years, with strong trunk that is now paralleled with small other trunks which were hanging aerial roots long ago. Its branches grew wider that the tree's shadow now touched the waters. It grew wider with more stretching arms like it can accommodate more spirits as the villagers believed. If it is true, can I find my father who left us eighteen years ago right at the same place. People don't want to disturb the tree for their own reason, but I don't wish to disturb it because it's just a tree.

The people here still believe that the dead spirits live on the banyan tree, yet they started sitting near the tree. Their belief hasn't changed, but the habit has.

Printed by Libri Plureos GmbH in Hamburg,
Germany